AND I HEARD_
A BIRD SING

ROSA GUY

LAUREL-LEAF BOOKS bring together under a single imprint outstanding works of fiction and nonfiction particularly suitable for young adult readers, both in and out of the classroom. Charles F. Reasoner, Professor Emeritus of Children's Literature and Reading, New York University, is consultant to this series.

Published by
Dell Publishing
a division of
The Bantam Doubleday Dell Publishing Group, Inc.
666 Fifth Avenue
New York, New York 10103

ISBN: 0-440-20152-7

RL: 4.8

Reprinted by arrangement with Delacorte Press

Printed in the United States of America

August 1988

10 9 8 7 6 5 4 3 2 1

KRI

"What's the matter?" Imamu asked.

"Chips," Margaret cried. "Didn't you see him?"

"So what?" Imamu asked. "He lives here, don't he? He works here. Why shouldn't he be?"

"He's not supposed to be here. He's not supposed to work here. Uncle James doesn't want him around. He terrifies me."

But Chips had lived there for years! At the hysteria in her voice, Imamu looked down at Margaret, puzzled. Was she all right? Did she, as Eloise Darcy had suggested, need therapy? Was she, as Amanda had hinted, acting just to get attention?

No, not the way she shook. Her fright was for real. "The kid's slow," he said, trying to reassure her. "He ain't dangerous." But Imamu thought of Chips's big, strong hands. He shook his head. Kids like Chips ain't dangerous. Had something happened between the two in the past that might have upset her?

"On my way out I'll tell Amanda that we seen him and where to find him," Imamu said. "I'll tell her to come out and sit with you."

"Imamu, don't go." Margaret held on to Imamu's hands. "Please, I'm always alone. I'm scared." He took her hands—helpless, begging hands—in his.

"I got to go," he said. "But I'll be back."

ROSA GUY is the author of *The Disappearance*, an ALA Best Book for Young Adults and a *New York Times* Outstanding Book of the Year, and *New Guys Around the Block*, both available in Dell Laurel-Leaf editions, and *Paris, Pee Wee, and Big Dog*, available in a Dell Yearling edition. Her translation of a Senegalese folktale, *Mother Crocodile*, was an ALA Notable Book. She lives in New York City.

ALSO AVAILABLE IN LAUREL-LEAF-BOOKS:

*To my niece Jean Ombwomeili and
to my little nephew Quasy,
our hope for the future*

1

Strange how constant his thoughts were of Charlotte Darcy. At every turn of his head, he saw again the gestures of her hands—how they commanded with their slightest movement—the turn of her head atop her spine, stiffened by pride. Her attitude came across as the gift of the haves, of course. To always have had. Imamu sighed, envious.

Sitting on his bed, in the silence between dark and dawn, he looked again into her eyes—blue, blue eyes. They had a way of looking at him—through him—as though searching into his soul! Crazy! What in the world did that elegant lady see in him— a delivery boy. Whatever, she liked what she saw, Imamu Jones was sure of that. It excited the hell out of him. And that was crazy too. The lady was old enough to be his mother!

And then, Imamu Jones thought about Gail Aimsley. He blushed with guilt. He tried not to think of her dark brown I-know-it-all eyes, their whites flashing bright against her dark brown skin. To think of her meant that he had to deal with her notion that nothing was so confusing it couldn't be thought out. A crazy notion. Perhaps. Perhaps he didn't want to think things out—when it came to Charlotte Darcy.

Sounds of his mother in the kitchen startled Imamu: The water running in the kitchen sink, her slippers brushing against the linoleum as she shuffled from sink to stove then to the round center table, forced him back to his responsibilities.

Imamu liked to think that he was always conscious of his mother's movements—at work or during sleep. It gave him comfort to know that she hadn't given in to her weakness and slipped off from their Brooklyn apartment to make her way back uptown to their old Harlem neighborhood. He worked better knowing the routine of her day: She awoke at dawn, sat in the darkened kitchen waiting for daylight, waiting for his first move to begin her day, then puttered around the house until he came home evenings.

Moma had her rights. If she wanted to leave, all she had to do was walk. A prisoner? Not his prisoner. After all, she was the mother—the grown member of the family.

These last seven months had been hard on her. Moving from their old neighborhood where the grooves of her life fitted the old apartment, the old neighborhood where they had lived since before his father had gone off to fight in Vietnam and been killed. In his eighteen years, Imamu had also fitted into those grooves. He knew what a gut-wrenching struggle it took to get out.

Stretching his six foot three inches up from the bed, Imamu crouched, shadowboxed, jabbed here and there, took his towel from the back of the chair, and walked back through his mother's room out the back door of their apartment and into the bathroom they shared with the other tenant on the floor.

Imamu hated sharing his bathroom. In their old apartment—in the bombed-out part of town, where addicts and winos clustered and where walking through the streets meant taking your life in your hands—they had had a private bathroom. Here, they paid more to live in the brownstone—a step up in the world, Ann Aimsley had said and he agreed—but they had to share their bath. Imamu got up early mornings to get in and out before the man next door stirred.

He didn't knock upward mobility. The streets were clean, the trees grew big and beautiful up and down them. Oh, for those trees growing in Brooklyn! He paused, thinking of the big tree spreading, almost like a gate, in front of the Maldoon mansion, Charlotte Darcy's home. An elm—the biggest and possibly the oldest elm tree he had ever seen. Looking up through its widely spaced branches, he could see to the second-floor window where . . . He blinked to get thoughts of Charlotte Darcy from once again claiming his mind. He stepped into the bathtub.

With the shower beating down on his head and shoulders, he gave himself over to a great feeling. Imamu had expected to miss his old Harlem neighborhood when he first moved to Brooklyn. He hadn't. Only good things had happened, and continued to happen, since they had come. He had liked the borough from the time the Aimsley family brought him there, two years before, as their foster child. Since then he had accomplished the impossible: He had brought his mother to this apartment; he had worked—was working—for the pleasure of living in a place that he had chosen, a goood feeling. From a street cat to . . . Imamu laughed up into the jetting stream—no limits. He didn't have to accept limits. He had a good job and the greatest boss a feller could have.

At eighteen he had nothing but time on his side. He paused in his vigorous soaping. What would it be like to be a child? He had never been a child. He had never had the care, the attention, given to other kids. Certainly he never had the care that he now gave to his mother. Did he resent it? Her? No. So why think about it?

But there had been a time when he had struggled hard against resenting her. When she had been out in the streets bending her elbow with winos, while he hung out—unnoticed, unprotected, getting in and out of trouble. But those times had passed.

If she hadn't been out there, then he might never have been Peter and Ann Aimsley's foster child. Even now, Gail Aimsley and her mother stopped by to sit with his mother—Mrs. Aimsley on her way from her volunteer social work, Gail on her way from school. Nevertheless, Imamu lived in constant fear: What if one day he came home from work to find her gone? Gail and Ann Aimsley might not always be able to mother-sit. What if, being lonely, Moma simply took the subway back uptown to be in the company of her old drinking buddies, sitting in the scooped-out darkness of one of those bombed buildings and had one drink and then another and another?

Imamu saw himself going to fetch her and her refusing to leave. He saw himself walking away, walking away, walking away. Would he just leave her to die? Would he be able to work again—feel free? Guilt. Imamu lived with the guilt of things he kept thinking, yet knew he would never do.

To change his depressing thoughts, Imamu turned the water from hot to cold. The tingling sensation restored his good feelings. Out of the tub, he tied a towel around his middle and walked back into his room. He dressed hurriedly.

In front of the mirror he patted his high Afro, and seeing strands of hair curling on his chin, plucked them out. He smiled, skinning his lips wide to see the effect of his white teeth brightening his already bright eyes, adding a glow to his handsome dark brown face. Then, pulling himself taller than his six three, he broadened already broad shoulders, looked himself over, and smiled. "Now I know why you catch the eyes of rich, elegant white ladies, you handsome dude you."

He pulled the bedspread over his bed but snatched it off when it didn't hide the lumps in the rumpled sheets. He didn't dare leave anything half done or undone. He never wanted to be the excuse for Moma to take the subway ride uptown.

Finished, he checked the room, then opened the door into the kitchen. Standing in the doorway, he looked at his mother, bent over her box of planted seeds on the windowsill. He noticed the way she prodded the dirt with timid, uninterested fingers. She kept trying only because of him. He kept impressing on her the possibility of her growing the perfect flower.

Seeing despair in her rounded shoulders, anxiety gripped Imamu. What if the thumb of an alcoholic succeeded only in changing seeds to dust? What if nothing grew in that box—ever? The world and all its ifs!

"Morning," Imamu sang out. "How we doin', Moma?"

Mrs. Jones jumped, startled. Tremors of self-doubt exaggerated the twitching of her face. She spread out frail, helpless hands. "Don't know, John," she said. "Ain't seen a thing—yet."

His mother had never been able to break her habit of calling him John instead of Imamu, the name he had given to himself. That was her way of being faithful to the memory of his dead father, John Jones. "Got to give 'em time, Moma," he said. "You just planted 'em."

"Over a week," she said. "And what about those others? Guess I ain't got no kind of thumb—green, pink, or purple. It's April. Things supposed to start growing in April. I waters them—good. The sun comes in that window all right. Mrs. Aimsley's been telling me what to do—but nothing . . ." She kept pushing at the dirt in the green box.

"In April things just get set to grow," Imamu said. "You hear tell about April showers—things like that? It's May when they come shooting out."

"I been reading up on 'em," she said. "Mrs. Aimsley brung the books for me to read. Ain't that something? How'm I gonna grow a perfect anything?"

Imamu went to her. He held her chin to keep the twitching muscles on her face still, then kissed her on her forehead. "Worry too much, Moma. I promise you they'll grow."

"Or like Gail says, we can always throw these out and start all over," she said.

"These'll grow," Imamu growled, angry at Gail. He shrugged. Gail might be right to leave his mother room for failure. "Anyway some flowers come out later than others. Some even come out in the fall."

"Don't know if I can go through the summer with nothing happening," she said. There was near panic in her voice that aroused an echoing fear within Imamu. What if his old friend Olivette's thinking was all wrong? Olivette said that folks—even ordinary folks—who worked hard could cultivate perfection. Surely Olivette had been the most perfect person he had ever known. Imamu had liked—no, he had loved—this friend, a new guy around his old block, so very much that indeed he had adopted his creed as his own. He believed it, or what was the use? But what if Moma wasn't even ordinary?

"Moma, if they don't grow I can always buy you some full-grown," he said, joking. "I'm a working man now."

"Go on with you," she said. She walked over to the stove to get the kettle. "You ain't nothing but a boy."

Imamu sat watching as she poured the water over the tea bag in his cup. He wanted to take the kettle from her shaking hands and pour it himself. But she had been trying so hard to be the mother. So he waited, keeping his eyes fixed on the pale, fragile hands. When she had finished, he said, "Moma, I never had a boss like Mr. McDermott."

"You ain't never had a boss before," she reminded him.

"That's right too." He laughed. Strange, in all the

years he had been out there, not going to school,
that this was his first job. The streets, juvenile
courts, jail—but never a job. In the tangle of his life,
he had just been an angry presence hanging on "out
there."

Now he worked as a delivery boy at McDermott's
Gourmet. He ate foods that he had never before
seen, hardly knew existed. His boss was the greatest.
It seemed impossible that any man could be as even-
tempered, calm, and honest as Mr. McDermott.
And he, Imamu Jones, was working for him and
being paid one hundred and thirty-five dollars a
week besides. Never had he made that kind of
money. Never had he thought of it.

"Gail says you oughtn't to be so satisfied with that
job," his mother said, as though reading his mind.
"Says they ain't paying you nothing. Says you being
glad to be there'll keep you from making something
outa yourself."

Imamu frowned. He wished that big-mouthed
Gail would stop that college hype on his mother.
Gail knew as well as he that he was doing the best he
could. How had she expected them even to get the
apartment, if he had had to depend on his mother's
veteran's pension? Getting up in the world had its
price. He didn't mind paying that price. He loved it
—enjoyed it.

Imamu looked around the large kitchen, with its
wooden cabinets that someone at some time had
paid good money to put in. He really dug the place.

When he got a raise, they had to move, but to another apartment with the same kind of cabinets—and a private bath. One step at a time.

"Gail ain't the one to decide," Imamu growled, reaching for a piece of toast.

"Don't you think that she ought to know, John? Being so smart and all?"

"As the world turns, Moma," Imamu said, grinning. Mrs. Jones walked back to the window to look down into the neglected garden of the street-level apartment below theirs. Imamu chewed hard on the cold toast.

The college girl and the delivery boy. That was the way Gail saw their situation. That's the way Gail got his mother—even in her permanently foggy state —to see it. The longer Gail stayed in college, the greater the distance between them. It had reached the point where Imamu refused to discuss things with her—especially his plans for the future. He didn't want to listen to her sounding off about her big ideas. Well, she had her dreams—and he had his.

Gail seemed to have forgotten that her father hadn't gone through college and her mother, who had, had married him. Peter Aimsley had earned his money as an auto mechanic and had saved up enough to buy out his boss. Now he owned his own auto-parts shop, and it was he who had bought the brownstone where his family lived, and had paid for Gail's college tuition.

Imamu drank his tea and went to the window to

stand beside his mother. Together they looked down at the twisted dried plants of other summers in the yard below. The garden apartment. That should have been the apartment where Moma started her experiment. He might have been able to help her with that one—help weed it. That garden had enough room so that if one seed didn't make it, another had to. That's what Moma needed—situations that guaranteed miracles.

"Got to go, lady," Imamu said, kissing the top of her head. "Be good now. If you can't remember, I'll be watching." Taking the bicycle from behind the door, he hoisted it onto his shoulders and made it down the stairs.

2

Imamu pedaled down the quiet street, nodding good morning to neighbors sitting on stoops or puttering around their front yards in the early morning. It pleased him how quickly he had adapted to country living. For whatever others might call Brooklyn, to him, it was country.

Dirty sidewalks had been his playground growing up, street corners his beat, until Ann Aimsley, for some reason, had seen something in him she thought worth saving. Most of the neighbors nodding to him as he rode by had first known him as the Aimsley foster child. Now he lived with his natural mother within calling distance from them. Neighbors had looked at him with suspicion when he first came. He had looked away from them with hatred. But that time had passed.

The tangle of life never ceased to amaze Imamu—the way an incident that on the surface had no relationship to another could be responsible for changing the other, completely. So crazy Iggy—his childhood friend—killing old man Fein, which might have sent Imamu to jail as an accessory, and into a life of crime, had by some circuitous route led him to a relationship with Mrs. Aimsley, involvement in the disappearance of her youngest daughter, Perk, and now, with his mother, to Brooklyn to his first job and a different life!

The Aimsleys had turned him around. And Olivette had opened up his mind to the possibility of perfection—even in himself. But it had been *his* decision to change his life—their lives. He had done it!

So whatever Gail Aimsley thought, Mrs. Jones's manchild had taken a giant damn step. And his next steps were going to be bigger and greater.

Imamu had never known happiness—never thought about it. Racing his bicycle through the streets before the start of early morning traffic, his chest expanded with pride. The morning belonged to him, the day, the weather—the too-hot-, too-dry-for-April weather that folks were grumbling about—belonged to him. The city tumbled to life because he, Imamu Jones, passed by. He held the magic wand that made all life possible. If someone happened to ask why he felt this way, his answer had to be: "Because I'm happy."

He wished happiness for everyone. He ached for

those missing out on it—like Margaret Maldoon, Charlotte Darcy's niece. Poor rich Margaret, paralyzed, condemned to a wheelchair, while living in what had to be the grandest house, on the greatest spot on earth. Margaret was unhappy. She had been happy once. Amanda, the cook, had told Imamu about it.

Did that mean the chance of being happy comes only once? What if it did and once lost never came again? Imamu let that thought encircle his mind, then shrugged. Couldn't prove it by him—he had never been happy before.

He arrived at the market early, but his boss was already there. "Good morning, Mr. McDermott," Imamu called out when he entered. The big, red-bearded man, raised his head from his order sheet on the meat counter to twinkle blue eyes at Imamu.

"And how's the laddie this lovely morning?" Imamu dug the Scottish accent his boss had cultivated to please his customers.

"Great," Imamu said. "Another hot day."

"That it is," McDermott agreed. "Seems someone up there forgot to turn the spigot to April." It had been warm in March too. The weather teased plants to early growth but made folks fearful of a drought.

Taking an apron from the stack on the counter, Imamu tied it about his long, slender body, looking at McDermott as he did, waiting. The man looked up, smiled, winked. Imamu grinned back with affection. McDermott went back to his order sheet.

Imamu took up the broom and began to sweep the floor.

The look, the wink—the no need for words between them—spoke of their closeness. Never had there been a man Imamu liked so well. From the first their friendship had had that texture: "You're a likely-looking chap," McDermott had said when he came in for the job. "Much quicker than your friend. Not that I fault the lad, mind you. Furgerson has a bit of a load to carry around, you must admit. Haha. But you now. Laddie, you have a build meant to get you places in a hurry."

McDermott had kept fat Furgerson on knowing his faults, which included overeating and laziness. Yet he had hired Imamu on Furgie's recommendation, when Furgie left to go back to school in the fall. That had made Imamu like him from the first. Since then, his feeling for the man, and McDermott's for him, had grown to affection and admiration.

"Laddie," McDermott said. "Will you be passing an eye over the pâté and cheese to see what we'll be needing?"

"Sure thing," Imamu said, putting aside the broom.

Sweeping floors wasn't one of Imamu's duties. Neither was being a stock clerk. Even getting to work early, he did only to give McDermott pleasure.

Imamu laughed at himself. He remembered the days he had sneered at friends, calling them Uncle Toms and handkerchief heads when he thought they worked too hard on their jobs. Now here he was working overhard, overtime, and from what Gail said, being underpaid.

To Imamu, McDermott seemed like someone from a faraway place who had nothing to do with whites in the United States. Certainly he had never known another white like him—in schools, in the Social Service Bureau, or the police stations, where he had had dealings with whites. Wherever McDermott had originated, had to be a place still to be discovered.

McDermott's customers all worshiped him. They came from miles around to his market. But then there were no greater gourmet shops for miles around. McDermott's carried the highest quality. All of which made the experience special. Imamu had never tasted gourmet foods before, nor had he ever known someone so trusted, admired, and respected.

The other workers began to come in. The telephone began its frenzied ringing. Imamu turned from checking the pâté and cheese to checking his order sheets. He filled boxes with fresh and smoked meats, with fruits, imported oils, and cheeses then went outside to hitch the delivery wagon to his bike. When he reentered the shop, McDermott called him.

"Laddie, Amanda the cook over at the Maldoon estate's on the line. She's ordered a few things she says she must have this afternoon. I hate asking—knowing how far out it is—but . . ."

Mixed emotions confused Imamu. He stilled the desire to shout, yes, I'll dash right out there. But on Mondays his mother expected him home early. On days when he had to be late he told her, told the Aimsleys. Then they came over to sit, or invited her over to dinner.

Imamu intended to keep things that way. He dreaded changing the sameness, the routine of their lives that kept him in control. To break it might give Moma excuses. He never wanted to give her excuses.

"But I deliver out there Thursdays, sir." And the orders were always more than enough to last them. To ride out there would take him more than two hours after he'd made his normal deliveries. The distance was great—so great that on cold winter days McDermott delivered their orders himself, after store hours.

"I know, lad, but old Mrs. Maldoon's had another stroke—last night. The cook is that distressed, don't you know. . . ."

"Another one?" Imamu said, feeling Amanda's distress.

Mrs. Maldoon, Margaret's mother, had been an invalid seven years before Imamu started working for McDermott. A stroke had left her paralyzed on her left side. Then in March, just around the time Imamu had begun to deliver, she had had another.

"In an emergency, laddie?" McDermott pleaded.

And Imamu argued to himself that loving folks carried its own demands. He said, "Do my best, sir."

"There, that's a good lad."

Satisfied that he hadn't actually promised, Imamu decided to go ahead with his normal deliveries first.

At four-thirty he called home to tell his mother he might be late. He let the phone ring only three times, then hung up, not wanting to disturb her if she was napping. He called the Aimsleys. There he let the phone ring a dozen times before hanging up. Upset by not making any contact, Imamu thought of going home. But fifteen minutes later he found himself riding full speed toward the Maldoon estate. He kept thinking of turning back. When he didn't, he decided that the trip was fated from the moment he had awakened in the morning, with thoughts of Charlotte Darcy filling his head.

The houses along the way were much larger than the brownstones where Imamu usually delivered. These houses had sprawling lawns where children romped and dogs ran around barking at strangers. A variety of hedges separated one house from the next, making each completely private.

Imamu delivered out in this section too—the Bay Mill section. He didn't like to. Unlike his regular route, where he charmed customers to fatten his tips, out here maids or cooks met him at back doors and handed him tips already decided by unseen, faceless people who felt that Imamu was paid to deliver—no matter the distance. That made him feel the underpaid servant. On the other hand, out at the Maldoon estate nobody ever offered him a tip and it didn't matter. Out there, Imamu knew he was liked and needed. Tips didn't pay for the pleasure that gave.

Dense woods lined the sides of the road between the last house of the Bay Mill run and the Maldoon estate. The woods formed a natural barrier against the outside world. A cacophony of insects, birds, animals, loud in the dank underbrush, underlined the loneliness and aloneness of the traveler. It made the distance seem endless. It had to be the longest, loneliest, scariest stretch on earth. Riding through it, the hairs over Imamu's entire body rose and stood at attention. Anxiety, fear, the feel of eyes watching from the underbrush, a sense of unknown, unseen things (people?), forced Imamu to bend over the handlebars and race.

Never did he look over his shoulder but kept racing toward one spot of light—a circle of light created by the tunnel of intertwining trees. Only when he came out into the sunlight could he breathe easy again.

His first journey out here, curiosity, more than any desire to please, had forced him on. Who were these people McDermott was so anxious to serve, even though they lived at the other end of such a nightmare? Now, Imamu raced ahead in anticipation. He, too, had become enchanted. What lay ahead pleased him—enriched his soul.

And as he gazed over the grounds spreading out before him, Imamu smiled—that mixture of relief and pleasure: the grass gleamed in the sun; the trees, their leaves and buds pushing out along branches that might have been staffs of gold. Even the air shimmering between sky and ground seemed to have been spun from the golden haze of sun. Bewitching.

The old rusted gates through which Imamu rode, symbols of once-upon-a-time, used to be opened by uniformed servants to let in the very rich, the powerful. Amanda had told him about that time. She had told him about balls given in the oversize foyer of the mansion. Dinner served in the big dining room —the table seating over a hundred guests.

Those were the days, Amanda had said. Even long after World War II the Maldoons had cooks working in the kitchen, two or three maids working in the upstairs rooms, and a housekeeper. Old Mr. Maldoon had had a butler, a secretary, and a chauffeur up until the day he died fifteen years before.

Now the only male working on the estate was the gardener, Giuseppe, whose mentally retarded son, Chips, lived with him in a cottage at the far end of the grounds.

As Imamu rode through the gates and up the narrow concrete path that led to the mansion, he saw Giuseppe—a tiny figure bending over in one of his gardens. He had many. Most were only recently overturned earth. But a few, he said, had already been planted.

On the opposite side of the road, the thick lawn— a sparkling carpet of green—rolled down and from a distance seemed to have merged back into the woods. But actually it ended at the edge of a deep ravine—at the bottom of which lay a large swimming pool already filled for summer use.

Braking as he came abreast of Giuseppe, Imamu dismounted and going over, stood looking down over the gardener's shoulders. Seeing flowers, where four days before there had been none, he said: "Man, what you do to get them flowers to grow?"

Giuseppe stood up stretching. He pushed back the old felt hat that shaded his face and smiled—a pulling back of lips to expose worn brown teeth, a face slipping into hundreds of tiny irregular lines, which smoothed out the moment the old man fell serious. "I plant the bulbs in the fall," he said.

"Since fall?" Imamu said. "And they only now growing out?"

"Tulips take time," Giuseppe said. He pulled out a soiled handkerchief to wipe the sweat on his tanned neck. He looked around the garden with pride. There were tulips of every variety, of every color, growing.

Imamu shook his head, kept shaking his head. Had his mother—Mrs. Aimsley—goofed by waiting too late to plant? What if his mother's seeds turned to dust again? Imamu gauged his concern for his mother by the deep despair that stirred within him.

Then he saw Chips, who had come to stand at his elbow.

Seeing the boy so close, without having heard him, startled Imamu. Nevertheless, he stuck out his hand. "Hiya, Chips."

Chips surprised Imamu by taking the hand. He pumped it up and down. In the months since he had been delivering at the estate, the boy had never approached him. Yet there he was, this six foot two inches, at least two hundred pounds of baby-faced manhood, trying to make Imamu's hand his own. What would happen if the kid really got to know him?

Imamu tried to pull his hand away, couldn't. He let it remain limp in the boy's hand. But Giuseppe turned to his son.

"Chips, what you doing here?" he asked. "What you want? You want Mr. Gleaner to ride by and catch you?" The boy let go of Imamu's hand. He looked around frightened. Then he hustled back to the obscurity of the back hedges. James Gleaner's name seemed to have that effect on the help around the estate.

Imamu flexed his fingers to get his blood circulating again. "What about flowers that don't need that kind of care?" he called back as he pushed off.

"All flowers need care," the old man said. "All plants . . ." Imamu didn't hear the last of his lesson, for he was using his energy to push up the incline and around the curve that brought him up to the three-story mansion.

The house, built of stone in the nineteenth century to resemble an old English manor, had been renovated through the years to reflect the luxury and comfort of modern times. But it still retained a castle-like quality making it the only house of its kind around these parts.

To Imamu it was impressive. The bigness of the place, its spacious lawn, even the woods that gave him goose bumps as he rode through, impressed with its majesty, its mystery.

Now as he rode around to the back door, he gazed up at the wooden shutters that closed in most of its empty rooms, the vines soon to be a curtain of leaves —and he noticed that here and there some leaves had already sprung to life from the pressure of the premature heat. New tendrils like worms searched for substance on which to climb. Imamu imagined the brown stone walls already covered with sheets of velvet-like leaves rippling in the wind.

He rang the bell at the back door. It opened instantly. "Oh-ho, so you get here at last?" Amanda—tall, heavy-chested, narrow-hipped, stood in the doorway pretending to be angry.

"I wasn't due back here again until Thursday," Imamu reminded her.

"Is true, sweetheart." The woman's West Indian tones softened and like magic her stern brown face did too—into an incredible handsomeness. "But I human, you know," she said, her voice plaintive, apologetic. "How I can remember all they does give me to do around here and still keep everything in me head?"

Taking the groceries from his cart, Imamu squeezed past Amanda, going into the small corridor that led to the huge kitchen. He put the bag on the long center table. Amanda followed, still complaining. "With the poor Mistress Maldoon sick, sick so—is a miracle she last the night, I tell you. And that nurse, Miss Norris, running like she ain't know she business and Miss Charlotte, sitting by the old lady bed like a statue—is me got to do all. . . ."

"She real bad off?" Imamu said. "Sorry."

"What to do?" Amanda spread out her hands. "Seven years the woman get her first stroke. She take to her room. Two months now she get the other, and take to her bed. And now again?"

"How is Margaret taking it?" Imamu asked. He held out the receipt for her to sign.

"Ask her self, nuh?" Amanda said. "She out front." Then she put her hand behind her instead of taking the receipt. "Eh-eh, but you in a rush? How? You just come."

"Running late, Amanda," Imamu said. Strange how his feeling for each member of the household differed. It all had to do with caring—on different levels. "Got a long way to go," he said.

Amanda opened her mouth in exaggerated surprise. She was a half-head shorter than he but appeared to be staring down over her hefty breasts at him. "But the girl outside waiting," she said.

"She doesn't know I'm here," Imamu protested. "I didn't even know I was coming. I come here on Thursdays."

"I tell her you coming," Amanda said. "The child lonely. Nobody take time with her. Look." She picked up a tray of fruit and pushed it into Imamu's hands. "Take this out to her for me, nuh?"

Imamu looked at his delivery on the table. He had never come out with such a small order. A cheap trick. He twisted his face to show resentment. But Amanda's way of conning favors from people—the way crooks conned money from the unsuspecting— amused him.

Seeing his suspicious look, she said: "Honey-baby. I know it's far for you. But what to do? Mrs. Darcy say she must have special olive oil for the old lady. I want bread and cheese and thing for the house. And the girl, she want to see you—bad. Go, talk to her a minute, nuh?" She nudged the tray of fruit in his hands and hustled him out of the kitchen and into the narrow corridor.

Imamu stood staring into the open door of Amanda's bedroom. He weighed whether he ought to take the tray back into the kitchen, put the fruit down, and go. It was unfair. Not only to him. More so to Margaret.

No matter how much she pleaded, he would have

to go. How stupid to go out to her, put the tray of fruit down on the table, and leave.

Nevertheless, he opened the door, walked across the hall toward the front door. His footsteps sank down into the thick oriental carpet and before he opened the door, he gave in to his desire to look around the hall at the portraits and busts of generations of Maldoons.

They awed Imamu, this preservation of folks' images in painting and sculpture meant to last forever. And why not? He who had no picture of his mother and only a vague recollection of his father and who rarely thought back to who had come before them, or about his forefathers. Why wouldn't he be impressed?

He recalled his first time in the hall. He had been looking at a painting—captivated by it—of a little girl dressed in blue. It was so completely of another time. The artist had captured the child's happiness, the way it had gone through her—from her feet, to her eyes, up to her wind-touseled blond hair. Charlotte Darcy. He had been admiring it when the voice from behind spoke. "Well—hello."

Looking around, he had known immediately that the woman coming down the stairs was the same little girl, grown. She wore the same color—blue—with the sure knowledge that that color was for her. Only now, her long-sleeved blue dress, cuffed at the wrists, was of a fabric that moved as her thin body moved. Her blond hair she wore twisted in a bun at the back of her head.

"What are you doing in here?" she had asked.

"Amanda asked me to open up the windows in the living room for her," he had answered, and she had laughed.

"Dear Amanda—up to her tricks. Don't let her deceive you. She isn't being as overworked as she'd have you believe." She had seen his apron. "From McDermott's?" And to his nod, her eyes—those all-seeing eyes—had gone over him and through him, making him feel his center.

She had pointed out the different likenesses of her family to him: the portrait of the first Maldoon who had come down from New England in the seventeenth century and had established his home on that site; the bust of her great-grandfather, who had been a great railroad magnate, as had been her grandfather, Daniel Maldoon the First, who had also been an ambassador to Britain. About the bust of her father, Daniel Maldoon the Second, she had said:

"He was a hard man. Uncompromising. Not necessarily brilliant." She spoke as though she had recently passed that judgment. "Just uncompromising." She had laughed. Then she had pointed to a painting of herself with her younger brother—a blond look-alike, Daniel Maldoon the Third.

Amanda had told Imamu about Charlotte's brother, Daniel, Margaret Maldoon's father. He had been killed in an automobile accident in Italy, the accident in which Margaret Maldoon had been crippled. And it had been Amanda who had told Imamu that the great wealth in which the Maldoons prided themselves had come from the railroad.

"Now, what do you think of my ancestors?" Charlotte Darcy had asked.

"Beautiful," Imamu had answered, meaning her. The meaningful smile in her eyes had deepened.

"Feel free to look around—whenever you wish," she had said. "This gallery used to be open to the public—once upon a time."

She had gone—faded really—up the stairs and into Imamu's mind.

3

Standing on the steps outside the front door, Imamu looked beneath the old elm tree at Margaret Maldoon in her wheelchair. She sat in the exact spot where he had left her on his last trips out. Why did someone, a young somebody—twenty-three—sit in the same spot every day? Did it make her feel more secure? He knew, even before crossing the narrow road to go to her, that he would find on the table a book facedown. She did read, that was obvious. But so slowly for someone who had nothing else to do— or did nothing else.

He had asked her about it, and she said she read in bed. Out under that big tree, she seemed unable to concentrate. Imamu believed that the book on the table was the same book he had found when he first came out in early March.

"Imamu!" Her pale eyes lit up when she saw him. "I was thinking about you—so very hard. I must have willed you here."

"Can't stay," Imamu said, hating to have to say it. Margaret liked and needed him. That was the reason, he guessed, that he liked her. "Amanda ordered some things. My boss asked me to do him the favor." He placed the tray of fruit on the table.

"Oh." The light faded, leaving her wide gray-green eyes haunted, sad. "I guess Amanda told you about Mother . . . ?"

"Yeah," Imamu said. He looked up through the spreading branches of the old elm, to the second-floor window. Sophia Maldoon's room. Charlotte Darcy spent most of her days there. The curtains hung still. "Sorry," he said, looking back at Margaret. "Know it's hard."

"It is." Margaret Maldoon nodded. She looked up at the window too. "I haven't spoken to my mother for seven years," she cried. "Will she die without forgiving me?"

Imamu remained silent. He had lived through times when he had imagined his mother dead without his seeing her or even knowing she had died. He had often envisioned visiting his old block, only to be told by some street dude: Man, they done shoveled your old lady off. That's why he had left the Aimsleys, who had given him a good home, and had gone back to her—and the streets.

"What can I do?" Margaret wailed. "She hates me."

Imamu had lived through that one too. His mother hating him, not wanting to see him. In Moma's case, Imamu had known it wasn't him. Moma hated herself, her own weakness—the bottle. He had done—was doing—for her what he thought might cure her of that hatred. But what could Margaret do?

"Naw," Imamu said. "She don't hate you—it's something else." But what did he know? What did he know about rich folks—rich white folks, and the way they thought?

Imamu looked down at Margaret. She sat hunched over in her chair. She wore a black-and-red-striped pullover that heightened her ash-blond paleness. Her thick hair was curly, beautiful—the one remaining feature of what Amanda had described as "a beautiful child—but a spoiled brat." Her eyes were large and round. They must have been attractive. But now they were too large for her thin face.

"The poor girl done pay twenty times over for being spoiled, though," Amanda insisted. "She just had to have her father take her to Italy for her sixteenth birthday, when she knew that her mother was sick, sick, sick. But that accident that killed him when he drove off that cliff is punishment enough."

"Please sit for a little while?" Margaret pleaded.

"My old lady's waiting," Imamu said. He looked

down at her hands. Their helpless look sent a thrill of anguish through him. He thought of his mother's hands. Did folks always give up on life through their hands first?

"Oh, Imamu," Margaret said, and shuddered. "I'm so afraid. . . ."

"Of what?" Imamu asked. His eyes went to the front door, which he had left open. He gazed at the busts of her ancestors outlined against the wall inside.

"I—I don't know," Margaret said. "I have this feeling of being watched."

Once again Imamu looked up at Sophia Maldoon's window. The curtains moved . . . Miss Norris the nurse? Charlotte Darcy? It certainly couldn't be Sophia Maldoon. She was too sick.

He looked back at Margaret. "It's because you're sitting here all day long doing nothing," he said. He glanced at the book lying facedown on the table. Then he looked away to the edge of the lawn, beneath which, in the dale, the swimming pool nestled. "Why don't you try swimming?"

"How can I?" Margaret said in panic. His suggestion sounded like a threat to her.

"If you can wheel this chair, Margaret, you can swim."

Imamu had known dudes from his old neighborhood who had only one leg, or arm—one had even been blind. They went swimming in the City Bath House, and had a hell of a good time.

"I'd be afraid," Margaret said.

"What of?" Imamu asked. "Didn't you ever swim?"

"Before. I—I was healthy then," she said.

"You're healthy now," Imamu insisted. "Except for your legs. All you have to is want to, Margaret. Just say to yourself I'm the most perfect swimmer and you can—you will."

"Stop trying to make a perfect person out of me, Imamu Jones. I'm imperfect. I always was—will always be."

"Stop feeling sorry for yourself, Margaret Maldoon," Imamu scolded her. "Just believe in yourself. Believe that you can achieve perfection and you can."

And as Imamu spoke, using Olivette's exact words, he felt gratitude that he had known the boy. Would he ever see Olivette again? Then he thought of his mother's seeds. They had to grow. The growth of those seeds would vindicate his friendship with Olivette—would vindicate his life.

He and Margaret kept gazing over the lawn, to its edge, fascinated. In some spots the drop was very steep, but for the most part the hill sloped gently down to the pool.

"Have one of your friends come over and take you down to the pool," Imamu suggested.

"I don't have friends!" Margaret Maldoon said, shrieking. For a moment Imamu imagined her the spoiled child, throwing herself to the ground having tantrums.

"Why do you say that?" he asked.

"I don't! I hate people feeling sorry for me! Everyone who comes here tries to feel sorry for me!"

"Sorry? Why sorry? Folks don't be feeling sorry for rich white girls." Even as he spoke his heart twisted in pain at her anguish. Guilty. He couldn't stop her self-pity. Guilty. He hadn't the time to try.

"I was—very good at most things," Margaret said. Pride sounded through those words—the way she said them. Imamu searched her face, trying to picture her arrogant, with vitality. But seven years of being an invalid had wiped away even the traces. "I did act . . . so sure of myself. My . . . Those who knew me were all glad that I . . . Anyway, I like being by myself."

Not true, Imamu wanted to say. Instead he said, "Why don't you ask Amanda to wheel you down to the pool?"

"Amanda? And have to listen to her complaints?" Margaret said.

"Amanda's got reason to complain." Imamu defended the woman who always showed so much compassion for Margaret. "She has this whole house to look after."

"Amanda's been complaining since Uncle James fired the butler and chauffeur," she said.

"Why did he fire them?" Imamu asked, remem-

bering the fear the man's name—James Gleaner—
aroused in Chips and Giuseppe.

"Since Dad died we haven't needed a butler or a
chauffeur," she said, defending her uncle. "Besides,
most of the rooms are closed. A woman comes in to
help Amanda with the cleaning twice a week. When
she or Aunt Charlotte needs something they call into
town—or my cousin Eloise brings it in from the city.
Have you met Eloise?"

"No," Imamu said.

"Aunt Charlotte's daughter," Margaret said. "She
—she's so healthy." She spoke with the envy of a
have-not, then changed her tone. "She's lovely—really lovely. She lives in town. Eloise is a scientist—at
the Cancer Research Center."

"Maybe she can come over to help you," Imamu
said.

"No! I—I wouldn't think of asking. . . . I—I
used to be so nasty to Eloise. She pretends she's forgiven me but I don't see how she ever can."

"Then ask your Aunt Charlotte," Imamu said.

"Aunt Charlotte? I can't. I'm so grateful just to
have her here. She looks so much like Daddy . . ."

"And what should she ask her Aunt Charlotte to
do that Aunt Charlotte hasn't done?" a voice asked.

The voice sent Imamu's heart skipping beats. He
heard Margaret answer, "I was telling Imamu how
good it is that you are here—with us."

Charlotte Darcy's eyes met Imamu's over Margaret's head. A wicked smile played just beneath their surface.

"I—I was just telling Margaret that maybe you could—could maybe help her out—swimming." He was stuttering, trying to force his breath to normal, trying to lighten his suddenly heavy tongue.

"Oh, but that *you* must do," Charlotte Darcy said. Her eyes were suggestive, but her face remained so calm that he questioned if what he saw in her eyes was real. "Margaret needs a friend—an outside friend," she said. "It would help her get her mind on other things. You must have heard how ill Margaret's mother is. And Margaret is so fond of you."

"Whenever I can," Imamu promised. "But I don't always have time—know what I mean?" Again her eyes deepened. Imamu's tongue grew heavy. "Was supposed to be here one minute, and already stayed twenty. Got to go."

He hated being unsettled, by anyone. Hated feeling the pigeon-toed, bashful kid, especially over an older woman. How old was she anyway? When he had talked about her and Amanda, to Gail, she had asked their ages. He didn't know.

Gail had said to guess. Look at the lines around their eyes, she had said, look at their necks—their hands. He had tried. But he never could look at Charlotte Darcy long enough. And Amanda? She belonged in the hall with the portraits and busts—forever preserved.

He waved, backing away, then, turning to go for his bicycle, found Charlotte Darcy walking beside him.

"Must you rush off?" she asked, her voice silky. "I had hoped you'd ask Giuseppe to cut some flowers for me. My room craves them. I just haven't had the time—there's never enough time."

"Flowers?" Imamu said. He hated that he sounded stupid.

Charlotte Darcy took a blue handkerchief from the cuff of her long-sleeved dress to wipe her pointed nose. She smiled. Oh, wicked, wicked woman, Imamu thought. Please don't do that to me.

"Never mind," she said. But her eyes kept holding their smile. "Let's make it another time. Right now, I have to spend all my waking hours with my sister-in-law. I guess Amanda has told you about poor Sophia. . . ."

Imamu nodded. Everyone had told him of Sophia Maldoon's stroke. But no one, not even a doctor, could tell him why giant beads of perspiration burst out all over him whenever he talked to Charlotte Darcy. Only when Imamu was back in the city, carefully maneuvering through the traffic, did he finally hear what Charlotte Darcy had actually said.

4

He hadn't called home.

He had had every intention of using the phone in Amanda's kitchen. Talking to Charlotte Darcy had pushed it from his mind; now, thinking of her kept it out until he had already passed the public telephones along the way.

Charlotte Darcy craved flowers. . . .

Around his old neighborhood, dudes were always talking about the older women who teased them, turned them on. Imamu had dug a few older ladies himself. But none had been so elegant, so rich. Even thinking of Charlotte Darcy—the blond lady with the wicked eyes—set his mind to churning, his body to burning.

And he kept forgetting to call home!

The shop was closed when Imamu arrived at

McDermott's. He chained the wagon to its post and walked to the nearest street telephone. He let the ringing go on and on, its echoes through the empty apartment strumming the anxiety at the pit of his stomach, like a bass.

What now? Her disappearing act? A trip uptown to find her? Then what? Imamu thought back to his days on the streets when his mind had gone around and around like a grinding machine—thinking of what to do about her, never stopping, never leading anywhere.

He rode home quickly, hoisted his bike to his shoulders, and went up the stairs, sensing the overwhelming silence awaiting.

The kitchen was dark. He stood, his back to the door, forcing himself to turn on the light. His gaze moved slowly around the kitchen. Gone? Skipped out? When? The moment he had left in the morning? Had she made it uptown?

Guilt: Whenever he didn't keep Moma uppermost in his mind, to protect her, something always happened. Despair: Did that mean that he must never go after the good life? That he was forever paralyzed —like Margaret Maldoon? Resentment surged through him.

His eyes rested on the telephone. He sagged against the door, relieved. Then, walking over to the phone, he picked up the note leaning there. Gail's handwriting: *Dinner at the Aimsleys—don't call. Just come.*

Imamu walked the few blocks to the Aimsleys' brownstone, his relief—and gratitude for having them close—so profound that by the time he rang their bell, his disposition had undergone a complete change. Happiness took over—completely.

Gail opened the door to his ring, scolding: "Well, it's about time."

A bolt of conscience reawakened his love. Imamu caught her tall, slim frame and held it against his. He loved the strong feel of her, her familiar minty breath. He tried to kiss her. Gail turned her cheek. Imamu chuckled. Recently she had been trying to change their relationship to a brother-sister bit. How? After two years of solid love? No way.

"We're already at table," she said, slipping out of his arms. "We tried to wait dinner but you were just too late." She headed for the stairs leading down into the kitchen.

Imamu stood, his elbow on the banister, watching her head bobbing down the stairs. Then he walked into the living room—with its lint-free carpet, its sofa and chairs forever new in plastic covers—to stand before the painting Mrs. Aimsley had given him.

At the time Mrs. Aimsley took in boarders, one of them, who had spent a lifetime painting it, had given it to her for back rent. Imamu had never forgiven them—the unknown boarder for giving, or Mrs. Aimsley for accepting it—even though it had been his gain.

The painting was Imamu's prize possession. He refused to take it back with him, when he went back to his mother, to their old Harlem apartment. Now he didn't think the brownstone where they lived to be suitable. Such a painting deserved a grand setting.

Taking a toothpick from his pocket, Imamu put it between his teeth. He stood biting down on it, waiting for the excitement the picture always created. The charging surf, the giant waves pulling little black matchstick figures laughing and crying into the darkened waters. Hundreds, perhaps even thousands of the little figures. The dude had put in some homework on that canvas. He ought not to have given it up—not for rent, not for food.

Working the toothpick around in his mouth, Imamu walked to the stairs, still feeling the relationship between the laughing, crying figures, with his moments of hopelessness, his moments of soaring expectations. He descended into the kitchen.

"There he is," Mrs. Aimsley said when she saw him. Her voice sounded her fondness for him. "There's our handsome, hardworking son, Mrs. Jones. I expected him to look worn out after those long hours. But he seems as fresh and as handsome as always. Come, Imamu, sit. I cooked your favorite today—lamb."

Imamu walked around the table to kiss Mrs. Aimsley. He brushed his lips to his mother's forehead, nodded to Peter Aimsley, then slipping into the chair next to Gail, squeezed her knee under the table.

"Took you so long," Peter Aimsley said, "we almost didn't leave you none. I was about to finish it all."

"No, you weren't," Imamu said, making a playful grab at the meat. "Not as hungry as I am. Haven't eaten all day."

He piled thick slices of lamb on his plate until Peter Aimsley shouted.

"Slow down, old buddy, that's enough already. Folks around this table's been counting on having seconds."

"Not this night," Imamu said, joking. "Everybody who thought that, is running in bad luck."

Cutting a piece of lamb, he put it in his mouth and closed his eyes, exaggerating. Mrs. Aimsley did cook good lamb—probably the best in the world.

He opened his eyes to look at his mother. "Hey, Moma," he teased. "Did you manage to pull a li'l something outa that box of dirt?" What a stupid thing to say. He realized his joke was a dud before her bland expression changed to one of embarrassment.

Dressed in a simple black dress, Mrs. Jones appeared almost normal. Only those who knew could see the tic in her cheeks—and her hands still shook.

"My God," Mrs. Aimsley said. "Must you put up with this needling every day? Don't let Imamu give you a complex," she said, and reached over to pat his mother's hand.

"I pays him no mind," Mrs. Jones said, a vague smile touching her face, which didn't register in her eyes. "He just talking to have something to say."

That touched Imamu. Her knowing that they had nothing really to talk about. How are you? How's your heart, still beating? he sometimes joked. Did Gail come over today? Did you talk to Mrs. Aimsley? How's that dirt box acting? Those were the little things that made up her life. He escaped every morning and came home to it every evening. A lifetime of knowing each other made it easy.

"What can you say to a son that can't even tell what time to get home?" Gail said. Imamu knew she was trying to annoy him. "After all, there is a limit on how seriously one takes a delivery boy."

"Gail!" Mrs. Aimsley's tone was sharp. "What a thing to say."

"Delivery or any other job got to be taken serious," Peter Aimsley growled. "Every little spoke keeps the wheel turning. Besides, he's doing all right. Or thinks he is."

Peter Aimsley didn't look directly at Imamu. The hostility that his foster father had shown when Ann Aimsley had insisted on bringing Imamu into their home, and family, had created a barrier between them. Even now when they had gone beyond hostility and had become friends, that first reaction remained the stumbling block between them.

"Now, when I started out," Peter Aimsley said. "Do you think that I—"

"Daddy, please, don't let's go through that again," Gail cut in.

"Yes, I will go into it, miss," Peter Aimsley said. "I started out as a car-repair helper earning fifteen bucks a week. I took that job serious. Now I own the joint."

"That—was another time," Gail said.

"No, that's anytime. Now, yesterday . . ."

"Why did I ever start?" Gail moaned. "Why can't I ever keep my big mouth shut?"

"I often wonder," Mrs. Aimsley said.

Imamu knew that Gail's criticism had been meant to maintain a big-sister attitude toward him. She wanted him to give up his job. She kept after him. He was pleased her father had stopped her.

"Yes." Peter Aimsley pointed his knife at Gail. "I respected fifteen bucks. Know why? Because I never questioned work so long as it was honest. So long as I could keep my mind mine. Keep my hands busy, and my mind free—understand? Stay healthy and keep planning ahead. That's important. Nothing stays the same, and when it changes, got to change with it. Know what I mean?" He shifted the knife toward Imamu. "Always be ready to jump from one rock to the next when the tide is swift, boy. Time goes on . . ."

"Dad-dy . . ." Gail groaned.

"Just you sit still and listen," her father barked.

He so seldom scolded her. Usually, Gail made him
—made them all—sit still and listen. "That's how
you got so you talk so much," Peter Aimsley said.
"Because of my thinking ahead. That's how you got
so educated. If I'd known you'd use my money to
try to outtalk every living . . ."

To keep from laughing, or agreeing, Imamu ate as
though he were starving. Gail deserved it. Ever since
she had decided to become a lawyer instead of a
fashion designer, she used her tongue as a weapon—
as though she had already made the bar.

Spearing a piece of lamb with his fork, Peter Aimsley pushed cabbage along with it and crammed it
into his mouth. He glared at Gail. She pouted. He
kept chewing, kept glaring. Gail kept pouting. The
table grew still. Everyone pretended interest in food.
All except Gail, who played with her fork, too upset
to eat.

Imamu glanced at her and seeing her dark, pretty
face, vexed, the sexy mouth poking out, worship for
her seized him. He pushed his knee up to hers to
show support. Then she shrugged: What can you do
with such people?

Imamu grinned. He read her mind. He liked to
read people's minds. He was good at it. That's what
had made him such a good detective. It came from
being out on the streets. Observing. Observing, without talking, could mean survival out there. If he had
money, he'd aim for being a detective, or better yet,
a psychiatric detective. Stop Gail from talking down

to him. But with him almost nineteen and her almost twenty . . . ?

The impossibility of his situation flashed across his mind—an unwanted image he blinked away. He'd luck up. As Peter Aimsley had advised, he'd keep his hands busy and his mind free.

"Had to make a delivery out to the Maldoon place this afternoon. That's what made me late." Imamu spoke to break the heavy silence settling around them.

"That's right," Gail said, deciding to forgo anger. "I haven't heard you mention them for days. Tell me, what are they up to these days?"

"Is that place still around?" Ann Aimsley asked. "I remember it well. Our teachers used to take us on trips to visit the historical old houses when I was a student. The Maldoon mansion was one of them. I remember hating to go out there. The woods were so spooky. . . ."

"It's still the same," Imamu said, smiling. He liked agreeing with his foster mother. He admired her. Loved her face, the way her whitening hair blended with the smoothness of her brown skin. A gentle woman. A great woman. Not perfect—just great.

"Those were some of the first Dutch settlements in Brooklyn," she said.

"Been lots of changes in those old places," Peter Aimsley said. "I've done work out that way. Houses changed hands. New folks done a lot of rebuilding—ranch-style, split-level houses—got lots of money."

"The old money is gone," Mrs. Aimsley said. "The old aristocracy doesn't exist anymore."

"Old money, new money, money's money," Peter Aimsley scoffed. "And what aristocracy? America never had no aristocracy—only crooks that knew how to make a buck. Believe the Maldoons made their money in railroad. Do you know the kind of killing that went down then?"

"What kind of money do you have, Mr. Aimsley?" Imamu asked. "New money or old money?"

"Honest money," Peter Aimsley said with a laugh. "That's the only kind of money that black folks got and that kind don't count a feller rich."

The answer surprised Imamu. He had always thought Peter Aimsley rich. Now he studied his foster father's face, noticed how furrowed his brow, its bristling eyebrows, the square jaw that gave the handsome face a look of strength, of substance. His glance fell to the squared tips of Peter Aimsley's fingers, the black lines beneath each fingernail that all the scrubbing never fully removed.

Imamu's eyes shyed away. His ears burned. Embarrassed. Why? Ashamed of himself? His foster father?

Then he heard Ann Aimsley. She was saying, ". . . the estate must take a fortune to care for—especially with today's cost."

But Peter Aimsley kept on with his line of thinking. "They kept us honest," he said. "Many a black man—and Chinese, too, got killed building that railroad. White folks, like the Maldoons, made the money. But it didn't make them happy. No sir. They got all that ought to make a feller happy. But they ain't happy."

"That's right," Mrs. Jones said, and hearing her, Imamu's embarrassment changed to anger. What did she know? What right did she have to sit there passing opinions—she whose life had been held to a standstill in the innermost part of the inner city? What did she know about what made or didn't make other folks happy?

His anger, pushing through him, spilled over across the table and went through her. She jumped. Imamu saw her jump. He saw the birdlike glances she darted at him, without even looking. Upset by his unreasonable anger, he turned it on Gail.

"So, that's what interests you? Big houses? You won't be satisfied unless you get one."

Gail waved him down, satisfied that for whatever reason, he, too, had been upset. "Oh, Imamu, you know me better than that. I've never been materialistic in my life."

Now, what did she mean by that? He'd be damned if he'd ask and have her bigmouth him. Then, annoyed with himself for having given her the opportunity to take over the conversation again, he shoved a forkful of food in his mouth.

The lamb was good. He put a forkful of cabbage

in his mouth. Mrs. Aimsley's cooking made the body feel good and satisfied the soul. No wonder he had this thing for older women. And as he ate, a warmth spread over him, dissipating his anger. When he had almost finished eating, he nudged Gail with his knee.

"Hey, Sis," he said joking. "That old job of mine might not be much. But it gets me money. I get paid on Friday. What say we take in a Saturday night movie?"

"Great," Gail said, her bright eyes teasing, a grin spreading out her face. "What about going into the city? I know where that old film *Casablanca*'s playing."

5

On Thursday, Imamu finished his regular deliveries before noon. He rode out to the Maldoon estate determined not to let anything interfere with the time he planned to spend with Margaret Maldoon, raced past the stretch of wooded road, his head down to escape the influence of its gloom. He turned through the gates then up the narrow road, stopping only to talk to Giuseppe.

"Giuseppe," he called out to the gardener hard at work in his garden. "Mrs. Darcy wants me to bring her flowers."

"Flowers? Mrs. Darcy?" Giuseppe frowned. He looked in the direction of the gates, through which Imamu had come, with deliberate suspicion.

"Monday, when I was here," Imamu explained. "She told me to get you to cut her some flowers." He stared unblinking into the old man's trying-to-be-wise eyes. Giuseppe shrugged. Going through the garden, he cut one here, another there, then handed Imamu the bunch.

Imamu rode on, pleased. At the back door, he took the box of groceries from the wagon and placed the flowers on it before ringing the bell.

Amanda opened the door, her mouth pruned with the gossip she appeared anxious to tell. "Oh, God, Imamu but what a night, you hear?" Then she saw the flowers. "Eh-eh, but what's this?"

Imamu placed the groceries on the table then handed the flowers to Amanda. "Tell Mrs. Darcy I brought her these."

"Who you say?" Amanda asked.

"Mrs. Darcy," Imamu repeated. "She asked me to —the other day. . . ." Imamu's voice trailed as Amanda snatched the flowers.

She took them to the sink and slapped them down on the counter. "Oh-ho, so she ask you? Well, let me tell you one thing, Imamu boy. Don't trouble your head trying to make no lonely, unhappy woman happy."

"Amanda, what do you think I intend . . . ?" Imamu asked.

"Me?" She shrugged. "I ain't asking. But it ain't for you to flower up this house. It's for me. For Miss Norris."

That pained him—having a wish unfulfilled, of having his gallant gesture misunderstood. Imamu watched Amanda as she unpacked the box of groceries. "Unhappy, Amanda? Is Mrs. Darcy unhappy?"

Amanda hunched her shoulders. "The woman alone. Her husband dead these ten years. And she loved the man." She glanced at Imamu. "A handsome man. A gentle man, you hear? Dapper, happy-go-lucky, a true British aristocrat. Too bad he was so poor. Her father didn't like him a-tall. Charlotte went on and marry him just the same. Now he's gone. Wasted up with liquor, don't you know. And she—she alone, holding she own hand. A woman bound to be unhappy so, ain't it?"

Once again she went through the groceries. "Eh-eh, but Imamu, you ain't bring the butter? And is butter I here waiting for."

Imamu checked his list. There was no butter on it. He held it out for her to see. "No butter here," he said. She looked away from the list.

"I know. I call McDermott after you had gone. But Imamu, upstairs, they need it. Ain't no butter as fresh as McDermott's."

The plea in her voice begged him to make the trip again. But he had deliberately come early to spend time with Margaret. Going back to McDermott's, then coming back, would make that impossible.

Seeing Imamu hesitate, Amanda said, "I hope you ain't think I can wait until next Thursday for butter?"

"It's a long way," Imamu complained.

"But the lady sick. They must have it."

"Okay," Imamu said. "I'll bring it back." Then as he opened the door to go, he asked, "Mrs. Maldoon doing okay?"

"Holding on," Amanda said. "Everybody waiting for the poor thing to go any minute. But is sickly people what know to hang on. And that poor old woman—I ain't know one day she well." Then as he stepped out of the door: "Oh, but I ain't tell you. What a night, last night, Imamu. Miss Eloise was here. Gleaner was here. They were sitting with Margaret. Then Margaret go to her room and what a set of bawling. You ain't hear nothing like it. Margaret swear somebody peeping in her window. . . .

"And don't you know, Gleaner say it Chips. He ain't like the boy a-tall. So he go to talk to Giuseppe. And don't you know, this morning the boy gone."

"Gone? Where?"

"Me? I know? Chips know Gleaner looking for him—so he hide."

"Why? If he ain't done nothing?"

"Imamu, the boy retarded. He ain't dumb. I know the boy. I look after him since the mother dead. He ain't a bad boy. But that Margaret—always looking for attention.

"That's what always was between Margaret and the mother—since Margaret was old enough to bawl. Pulling at the father, making him take her here, take her there, take her everywhere. Leaving poor sick Sophia alone, heartsick. Young Daniel, never know what to do, poor man. He was nice—but too soft, you know."

"How is Margaret now?" Imamu asked.

"Oh, she all right." Amanda gave a dismissing movement of her hand. "She out there with her cousin Eloise."

Imamu left the house and walked around to the front to talk to Margaret. A loud gust of laughter greeted him as he neared the big elm—the kind of laughter that meant, he hoped, that Margaret had recovered from her fear. But when Imamu cleared the tree, he saw Margaret sitting hunched over at the table, clasping misery to her bosom.

In contrast, Eloise Darcy—blond hair, blue eyes, standing six feet tall, wearing a white laboratory coat that spoke of her imminent departure—looked refreshingly alive, capable. Seeing Imamu, she put out her hand and caught his in a firm handshake.

"What a handsome young man," she said. "Now I see why Margaret's been waiting for you with such impatience."

Imamu liked her. He hadn't known what to expect of Charlotte Darcy's daughter. Certainly not a woman who already was in her thirties. Nevertheless, there was something about her clear, see-through eyes, their projected openness, honesty, that made Imamu want to return her compliment. He wanted to say, "You're gorgeous too," and see the blue light up with the same pleasure that her words had caused him. He wished he could be honest, that he had said to Amanda, in the kitchen, Yes, I got the flowers for Charlotte Darcy, because she wanted them and I wanted to bring her what she wanted. He had not because he dared not.

Honesty had to be weighed against background—his life on the streets; being black, being a delivery boy. With sudden clarity, Imamu saw how impossible it was for poor folks to be completely honest. Only those in control—of money, education, themselves—could afford that kind of honesty. He stood staring inside himself, amazed. He had just learned a lesson.

"Glad to meet you, Eloise," he said. "We were talking about you—Margaret and me. I was telling her that maybe she ought to ask you to help her—take her down to the pool, help her to swim."

"Imamu," Margaret wailed, embarrassed. But Eloise Darcy's face lit up with pleasure.

"A wonderful idea. Margaret, that would be just the thing—something that we can do together. I want us to."

"Eloise, you don't have—you mustn't." Margaret's pale face flushed a light pink.

Eloise laughed, relieved. "I'll work it into my schedule. It's only April. It will get colder before it's summer. Why don't we plan on devoting our entire summer to it?"

"That will mean you have to come out here every day," Margaret said.

"That's why they make cars, Margaret. So busy people can accomplish the impossible."

"See," Imamu said. "All you had to do was ask."

"What do you do, Imamu?" Eloise said.

Imamu flushed. Was she putting him on? She had to have seen his apron, even if Margaret hadn't told her. "I work for McDermott," he said. He expected to feel his usual surge of pride. He didn't.

"I mean apart from that." Eloise waved her hand at his apron. "You're much too handsome and intelligent to be just a full-time delivery boy. What school do you attend?"

"None," he said. "I dropped out."

"When do you expect to drop back in?"

"Don't know." Imamu shrugged. He didn't go in for this unyielding candidness. "Been in a li'l trouble —know what I mean? Right now, my old lady got to be looked after. She's sick."

"Your mother? Aren't you too young to have that kind of responsibility?"

"My old man's dead," Imamu said, and wondered how she was able to get him talking about himself. "All she got's me."

"What about public assistance?"

"My old man was a vet," Imamu said. "She gets a li'l pension. But that li'l money . . ." He shrugged again. "And—well, those who put me out of school ain't exactly waiting for me to come back."

"What a terrible system that keeps young people out of school because of a little mistake."

"Guess it was lots of li'l mistakes," Imamu admitted, grinning. As he said this the thread of his reeling thoughts forced his eyes to gaze over the endless expanse of lawn.

Growing up in the streets, the way he and his friends had to, mistakes had been a natural way of life. They were born to it. Living one snatch outside the law made them many snatches away from Eloise Darcy's kind of honest life.

Chilled by this reality, Imamu's fingers went for a toothpick. He put it into his mouth and moved it around with his full lips, still gazing at the sunlit green.

Even the sun favored those who had everything. Eloise Darcy belonged to that breed favored by the golden sunlight. She might live miles away in Manhattan, but this estate was hers to take in her six-foot stride. Honesty had been handed down to her in that gallery which kept her grans, her great-grans preserved. It had been willed to her from birth. Only the greatest of human tragedy would have deprived her of . . . That thought brought Imamu's eyes back to Margaret, hunched over in the wheelchair.

"You must go back to school, Imamu," Eloise said.

"It ain't easy," Imamu answered.

"It's never easy," Eloise Darcy said. "It takes hard work to maintain a sound and balanced mind."

With those words she erased all distance between them. Gail said the same thing. Gail kept harping away at it. But Gail made going to school—starting over again in a sense—sound easy. Eloise Darcy had agreed with him: It was damned hard.

"It's wonderful of you to take time with Margaret," Eloise said. "I have been trying to talk her into going somewhere where there are people—lively people, to keep her company. She doesn't want to. My mother agrees with her."

"What she's trying to say, Imamu," Margaret said, "is that I need to go to a place—to get therapy."

"Maybe all you need is Imamu." Eloise smiled. "And me. I must go now. Are you ready for a lift back to town, Imamu?"

Imamu shook his head. "Got my bike," he said.

He watched her walk over to the little Volkswagen Beetle parked behind a brown-and-tan Mercedes in front of the house. He liked her walk. Her swaying hips, the way her long hair hit at her shoulders. She had her mother's complexion, yet they were so different—in looks, in manner. He looked up at the window of the sick woman's room. The curtain moved. Imamu smiled.

"You shouldn't have asked her," Margaret spoke up after the Beetle had driven away. "She agreed only because she's sorry for me."

"No," Imamu said. "She agreed because she agrees."

"You heard her. She keeps talking to Aunt Charlotte to have me sent away. She thinks I need therapy."

"She wants to help you," Imamu said.

Margaret hung her head. "She is kind to me. Too kind. She has so much to forgive me for. I—I used to be terrible to her. She never talks about it." She sat quietly for a second. "I'm glad she doesn't. Having her and Aunt Charlotte around makes me feel as though I still have a family."

"Oh, come on," Imamu said. "Your old lady ain't dead neither."

"No—not yet." She gripped her arms and looked up at the window. "Will she die without forgiving me? I was so young, Imamu. Sixteen is young!" She opened her hand in a helpless gesture. "Why should she? I can't forgive myself—ever!"

"Margaret, maybe you ought to go away," he said. He, too, looked up at the window. The curtain hung still. "Maybe to an institution, a school where—"

"No!" she shouted. Her face grew pink again—this time in anger. "I was born in this house! My father was born in this house! This is where he grew up. This is where I want to be!"

Do you intend to die here too? Imamu wanted to ask. Then he remembered Charlotte Darcy, speaking as though those in the paintings, the bronzes, were living still.

Imamu let his gaze go over the grounds that the sun had chosen to favor. A squirrel stood on its hind legs nibbling at something in its front paws. Birds pecked here and there in the green. He gazed over to where the lawn seemed to merge into the woods, but where in reality it sloped down to the dell and the pool lying—large, lazy, tantalizing as a lover—waiting to be used.

Why leave? If he had all this going for him, would he leave? Where to go? And as he stood considering a prospect that even in his fondest dream he had no possibility of having, Margaret gasped. Imamu looked at her, then in the direction where she was pointing. He saw a figure in the shadows of the woods. Chips? But even as he looked the figure stepped back to be absorbed by the shadows.

"What's the matter?" Imamu asked.

"Chips," Margaret cried. "Didn't you see him?"

"So what?" Imamu asked. "He lives here, don't he? He works here. Why shouldn't he be?"

"He's not supposed to be here. He's not supposed to work here. Uncle James doesn't want him around. He terrifies me."

But Chips had lived there for years! At the hysteria in her voice, Imamu looked down at Margaret, puzzled. Was she all right? Did she, as Eloise Darcy had suggested, need therapy? Was she, as Amanda had hinted, acting just to get attention?

No, not the way she shook. Her fright was for real. "The kid's slow," he said, trying to reassure her. "He ain't dangerous." But Imamu thought of Chips's big, strong hands. He shook his head. Kids like Chips ain't dangerous. Had something happened between the two in the past that might have upset her?

"On my way out I'll tell Amanda that we seen him and where to find him," Imamu said. "I'll tell her to come out and sit with you."

"Imamu, don't go." Margaret held on to Imamu's hands. "Please, I'm always alone. I'm scared." He took her hands—helpless, begging hands—in his.

"I got to go," he said. "But I'll be back."

"When?"

Imamu thought of the trip to town, the long trip back. "Later," he said. "I got to get Amanda some butter."

"Promise?" She held on to his hands, pleading.

"I promise, I promise. What to do on Thursday afternoons if I don't sit with Margaret Maldoon?" He grinned as he tried to disengage his hands. But then a voice spoke from behind him. At the same time a hand came down on his shoulder.

"What's this boy doing here?"

Imamu didn't like the tone of the voice, and when the hands spun him around, he didn't go for that action either. Nevertheless, he gave the tall, handsome man time to look him over, time to let him see he was no boy. And he studied the man—the black hair graying at the temples, the fit of the well-cut, dark blue business suit.

"I want to know what he's doing here." The man had balled his hands into fists.

"Uncle James, this is Imamu Jones. He's my friend."

The gray eyes, under shaggy, black eyebrows and thick black lashes, blazed. "Tell him to go," he said.

Imamu had heard about James Gleaner, Sophia Maldoon's older brother. He hadn't known what to expect, but he surely hadn't expected this man—in his late fifties or early sixties—ageless, and so well built. Whatever his age, Imamu had no intention of standing still to be socked, stomped, or insulted.

"Get out," James Gleaner said, pretending that he hadn't heard Margaret. "Deliveries are made through the back door. The same road that leads to that door, leads back to the gates. I don't want to see you around these grounds again."

"Look, man . . ." Imamu said, thinking it better to explain.

"Don't let me have to throw you off," Gleaner warned.

The man thought he could. Obviously he had spent time in the gym doing judo, or some such thing, to keep him in courage. But Imamu had no intention of being thrown or even touched by the turkey. A dude who carried prejudice like weights had to waltz to the end to get a move out of him.

Imamu kept saying to himself: Man, you were leaving. Why don't you just go?

The two thoughts were slugging it out in his head when he heard Charlotte Darcy say: "James, do you really think it's a crime for Margaret to be talking to a boy?"

"Keep out of this, Charlotte. I'm the one who decides who has access to these grounds."

"Don't be an ass, James," Charlotte Darcy said. "The boy's not going to rape Margaret just because he's talking to her."

"He's my friend, Uncle James," Margaret repeated. "My only friend."

Ignoring Margaret, James Gleaner kept staring at Charlotte. "What do you know about these people?" he asked.

"All kids are not necessarily like the ones you grew up with on the Lower East Side," she said. "This is another time—another place."

"What do you know about those times, Charlotte? Sophia likes to ramble but she's never been an accurate storyteller."

Charlotte Darcy laughed and the air crackled with their hatred of each other. "Sophia's not rambling now, is she James? She's always asleep. Not being able to hear her ramble is driving you quite mad."

They kept staring at each other. James Gleaner bristling. Charlotte Darcy containing her hatred, just beneath the facade of a smile.

"Charlotte," James Gleaner said. "I don't intend that my demands be ignored."

"You are so primitive, James," Charlotte Darcy said. "I often wonder how you and my brother Daniel ever became friends. Daniel was so different. He might have been weak but he was such a gentle— person."

Her tone, her attitude conveyed contempt. James Gleaner's nostrils whitened.

"The difference, Charlotte, obviously didn't work in your favor," he answered, and turning from them, walked away. He got into the brown-and-tan Mercedes, slammed the door, and raced off. The others watched motionless, listening to the angry motor racing, long after he had gone.

Then Charlotte Darcy said to Imamu, "Don't mind James. He's never outgrown his hatred of blacks. They used to beat him up after school in his old neighborhood. Now he can't stand the sight of them. He believes that where you see one, you're bound to see others."

Imamu felt his face flame. Like cockroaches? he wanted to ask. He hated her. "I was only talking to your niece," he said.

"I saw you," she said. "That's why I came down." She took her little blue handkerchief from the cuff of her sleeve and wiped the tip of her nose. The smell of lavender, wafting beneath his nose, forced Imamu to turn away. "I'm leaving," he said, and walked away.

"Imamu, you promised . . ." Margaret called after him. But he didn't turn. He refused to turn. But Charlotte Darcy followed. And when he had mounted his bike, she held the handle.

"Don't go away angry, Imamu," she said.

"Look," Imamu said. "You don't know me. Neither does that dude. I don't be standing around letting folks talk to—or about—me any way they want."

"Oh." She waved a hand. "James can't have it both ways. He can't squeeze the life out of the house with his economy then deny us a chance to breathe. At any rate, he's seldom here. Don't let this keep you away from . . ." She paused, smiled. ". . . Margaret."

6

Angry, Imamu rode through the gates, muttering: "I don't have to take that crap. Giuseppe's suspicious looks, Gleaner's smut. Charlotte Darcy—Charlotte Darcy . . . Does she think I'm a kid just out of Sunday school? She sure got another thing coming."

He raced down the long stretch of wooded road, in a rage that blinded him to the animals darting across his path and scurrying into the underbrush.

Margaret Maldoon, needing him. Begging him. What was a rich white girl doing needing him! So she was scared. So she was unhappy—and an invalid. Nasty as she was accused of being, when she could walk chances are she would never have even talked to him. Now she called him "my friend" to her loving uncle. Well, let Uncle James sit and hold her hands. McDermott could get another boy for that long run. If not, let him take his job and shove it.

Meanness made Imamu light-headed. It set him free. He raced out past the forest, through Bay Mill, pebbles spinning, animals scattering out of the way of his reckless wheels. He had worked hard, acted the square, grinning to please—a bad dude gone respectful. Now this turkey, a fugitive from an outdated slum, steps into his life and tries to turn the clock back on him.

Turning into the main street, Imamu swerved to keep from being hit by a two-tone tan-and-brown Mercedes racing toward him. The car flashed by. Imamu caught a glimpse of the face at the wheel. The face of the man uppermost in his mind.

Half an hour later, he entered the gourmet shop hot, dirty with sweat, and still angry. McDermott, standing behind the meat counter disjointing a side of veal, looked up. "Well, laddie," he said, wiping his hands on a towel, then putting them on his hips. "It's a bit late that you're getting back, isn't it?"

"Got held up," Imamu said. But he wasn't late. If anything he was early—much earlier than usual.

"And you got yourself in a bit of trouble, too, now, didn't you?" McDermott asked. Imamu saw again James Gleaner's angry face bent over the wheel of the two-tone car.

"I didn't do nothing wrong—sir," Imamu said. "I was out at the Maldoon place and was talking to—"

"That's not what you're supposed to be doing,"

McDermott said, and Imamu's scalp crawled. A hot flush sent blood racing to the back of his neck. He wanted to say: I did my work. I made my deliveries. I earned the time to stand and talk. Instead he took a toothpick out of his pocket and put it into his mouth.

"I said—I was talking, Mr. McDermott." He spoke calmly yet anger crept into his voice. "I'm not supposed to talk?"

"That's not what I pay you for now, is it?"

"What do you pay me for if it's not to be polite?" Imamu asked. "I deliver groceries—I'm polite."

"Oh? Polite now, is it?"

McDermott stood before Imamu, hands behind his back swaying like a schoolteacher giving a bad boy hell. But his eyes without its twinkle were like two glass buttons stapled to their whites. "And does polite include holding hands and walking about private property making a blooming nuisance of yourself?"

"Mr. McDermott, you didn't ask me if I did that," Imamu said, returning McDermott's stare. He felt something in their relationship changing. He struggled for it not to change. He wanted to see McDermott the way he had seen him earlier, the way he had seen him since he had come to work for him. It was important to Imamu that that feeling never change.

"Well, did you or didn't you?" McDermott asked.

"Do you think that if I was holding Margaret

Maldoon's hands it would mean I wanted to rape her?" Imamu asked. McDermott's eyes shifted.

"Oh, never mind," he said. "I guess Gleaner might have seen things not there. Not to worry. You won't have to go back. I'll be getting a new boy to work that route."

"Why?" Imamu asked, forgetting that he had reached the same conclusion earlier. "I didn't do nothing wrong—Gleaner knows that."

"But he's the customer, lad," McDermott said. "And you know what they say? Customers are always right."

"I don't care what they say," Imamu said. "The dude's way out, wrong. And you can't make him right by keeping me away."

"I hear what you're saying, son," McDermott said. "But what can I tell you? That's the way it is."

"It?" Imamu asked.

"Life, son—life."

"Life? That you can trust a new boy you never met more than you can trust me?"

"Look at it this way," McDermott said. "It's quite a way out to the Maldoon place. Be glad you don't have to make that trip every week. What with your mother and all." But as he spoke McDermott's eyes shifted, kept shifting. That was the first time in the seven months since Imamu had come to work for him that McDermott couldn't look him in his eyes.

Butter. A pound of farm-fresh butter. Imamu lay still during his first waking moments. Dread held him, held his eyes closed. A pound of butter? Through his expanding thoughts he knew. He held on to the promise he had made Amanda for another reason.

Slowly, Imamu awakened. And as he did he remembered—promises. The wider awake he became, the more important the promises grew: the butter for Amanda; his promise to come back that he made to Margaret. He had failed her—poor lonely Margaret who trusted him. He hated to break a promise. He was a man—had grown to be a man of his word. . . .

Then he thought of McDermott. Imamu jumped out of bed. He rushed to bathe, to dress, to be gone from the house before his mother stirred.

Racing through the dim, almost deserted streets, he arrived at the shop before his boss and waited impatiently until he drove up. "Well, laddie," McDermott said, opening the gates. "I see you're making it out before the birds."

From his tone, McDermott seemed to have forgotten their exchange of the day before. But as Imamu was tying on his apron, he twinkled his eyes to say: "We're in luck, laddie. I found the boy who's going to take over your run out Bay Mill way. We have enough to keep us busy around town, wouldn't you say?"

Imamu turned from the wink, the smile. Would he

see that face tomorrow the way he had seen it yesterday? He found it impossible to pick up the broom to sweep the floor. Instead he busied himself checking over his order sheet, remembering to take a pound of the country-fresh butter Amanda had requested from the dairy case.

Friday. A busy day. Dozens of orders to fill. Without thinking it out, Imamu knew his first stop. Long before the market opened for business, he was on his way out of town. As he rode through the early morning, Imamu reflected that the trip had as much to do with his feeling for himself as it did with promises he had made. He had been trying so hard to build pride in himself, his honesty, his ability to keep his word. It seemed to him that never could he be honest again, if he let a cat named James Gleaner—or a McDermott—cheat him of self-respect. He had earned it—and other folks' respect too. Never did he want to be without that.

Later he intended to explain to McDermott that he had delivered the butter to the Maldoon estate, against his wish, because he had given his word. If McDermott fired him because of that, nevertheless, he, Imamu Jones, would have the satisfaction that he was a dude who could be depended upon.

In the early morning, the woods were darker than he had ever seen them. The darkness made the narrow road narrower. It crowded Imamu.

Silence. A waiting silence—animals, birds, insects, all waiting for the seeping light to break through to

overwhelm them. The silence, the dark, was like a
giant hand heavy on Imamu's shoulders. It slowed
his legs and made him think longingly of the terrible
anger of the evening before that had whizzed him
aggressively through the detested stretch. But now,
using all his strength, he was barely able to pump, so
that the bicycle wobbled first to one then to the
other side of the road.

Looking ahead at the circle of light—now gray
instead of gold at the tunnel's end—it seemed far
away. When he had ridden midway, it seemed to
him he still had forever to go.

Finally he rode out into the soft morning light.
But strangely enough, he had brought along his fear.
And as he went up the narrow concrete path, he
kept looking around, as though for enemies hiding
over the silent grounds. Imamu's heart kept pounding and he kept asking himself: What the hell are
you scared of, fool. You made a promise. Promises.
And you are here—late as hell, but just the same,
you made it.

Still, he knew that early as it was, there was
hardly a chance that Amanda might be up, and less
of a chance that Margaret would even be around. So
he had kept his word. So what?

And the stillness spreading over the grounds, the
mist shrouding the mansion, forced him to tiptoe.
He tiptoed to the back door and, terrified of shatter-
ing the silence by ringing the bell, put the butter
where there would be shade on the windowsill in-

stead. Then he walked to the front of the house, jumpy, impatient. Impatient for the sun to shine, bright, brighter. He needed every bit of light to make it back through that long, lonely wooded stretch.

Walking up to the big elm tree, Imamu leaned against it looking up at the sky, then over the wide expanse of lawn, longing for its golden hue. He looked up at the second-floor window. Had the curtains moved?

Imamu shook his head, and despite his uneasiness, he chuckled. "Believe what makes you happy, Imamu Jones." The curtain hung still—still. Restless to be gone, yet wanting to wait for life to begin in the mansion, he strolled across the lawn, testing the thick grass beneath his feet, enjoying the moist feel of the morning dew. At the edge of the lawn, he gazed down the slope at the pool—dark blue in the early morning light—in which an object floated.

Trying to make it out and not able, Imamu sauntered down the hill, noticing as he went how well Giuseppe kept the green, so perfect that a scrap tossed in its path glaringly disturbed the tidiness. Imamu picked up the scrap. A handkerchief. Charlotte Darcy's embroidered blue handkerchief. He held it to his face, letting the lavender fragrance invade him. He looked back at the silent house, tempted. Shaking his head, grinning, he muttered, "Don't you be no fool, Imamu Jones."

Taking out a toothpick, he put it in his mouth and, still chuckling, continued down to poolside.

There he stood looking at the floating object, absently, still caught up in the humor of his crazy temptation. His heart constricted. Something familiar about the object claimed his attention. Something terrible. But why? Red and black stripes? The red, dark from the water, but the same bold stripes!

Margaret? What the hell was she doing? What was she trying to prove? She couldn't swim! And as one unreasoning thought raced after another through his mind, Imamu found himself in the water swimming out to her. He grabbed her arm, and immediately wanted to let go. But nothing he wanted seemed within his possibilities. He swam to the side of the pool, climbed out, dragged her from the water, pulled her to the grass beneath a tree, pressed down on her back in an attempt to empty her lungs. He turned her over, bent over to give her mouth-to-mouth resuscitation. His being rebelled. No! He could not! He could not touch her. Never! Never again could he touch that cold, hard body! Imamu backed away. He kept backing away—then he turned and bolted.

7

A strong breeze took the bicycle. It flew through the air. Wind blew in Imamu's face, sang in his ears, holding him on a threshold between dream and reality—numbness and the turbulence of a nightmare. A consistent honking of a horn forced Imamu to swerve from the wheels of a trailer, and brought him back to consciousness. Maneuvering in the flow of traffic, he slowed down. Darkness lifted from his mind. He thought of McDermott.

He had defied McDermott. Why? McDermott had always been in his corner. Why had he awakened this morning, defiance like a flag waving over his intentions. His boss, his boss, his boss. He had to explain? But what? He had to apologize. What for? What had he actually done? Whatever, he had to talk to McDermott. But in cold wet clothes? Imamu shivered.

His bicycle had been racing on its own. Now it veered toward home. Leaving it at the curb, Imamu ran upstairs into the apartment and into his room. He changed clothes hurriedly, then rushed out only vaguely aware of his mother sitting in the kitchen.

On the street, feeling calmer, he delivered the groceries he had taken from the shop earlier. But as he went from place to place his thoughts stayed with McDermott. What to tell this man, whom he dug the most? His mind once again went blank.

Midafternoon when Imamu walked into the shop, two men were talking to McDermott. Detectives. He could tell them anywhere. Imamu had spent his young life spotting them.

Ignoring them, Imamu went to the counter, pretending to be interested in the delivery sheets. But McDermott called, "What's this about butter, laddie?"

"Butter?" Imamu said, not understanding. "What butter?"

"See," McDermott said. "My boy delivered out there yesterday. He's been delivering in town today."

"Just repeating what the cook said," one of the men answered. "She claims the boy promised to bring the butter last night. And that this morning she found it on the windowsill."

"Been an accident out at the Maldoons'," McDermott explained. "They think that maybe you might know something. I told them impossible."

"If you didn't take the butter out there today, when did you take it?" the detective asked Imamu.

Imamu looked at the men, then from the men to McDermott. They waited for his answer. The butter? The butter? Yes, he remembered the butter. He had put it on the windowsill. He tried to remember. He had walked to the front of the house. He had been waiting for the sun—the sun . . . Suddenly the entire scene flooded his mind. Margaret was dead! He had taken Margaret Maldoon's corpse from the pool. It had been cold, hard. He had bent over her, wanting to put his mouth against her dead mouth. He shuddered. The men saw him shudder. They looked at him, waiting.

Margaret Maldoon is dead!

He had run. Why? What if he had been able to save her? He couldn't! Margaret Maldoon was dead! He should have gone to Amanda. But Margaret Maldoon was dead! What about his word? His self-respect? What did all that matter to these men? Margaret Maldoon was dead, drowned. And he, black boy, had been out there in the early morning without reason. He had no real reason that they would respect. McDermott had taken away his reason.

"When?" one of the detectives asked suddenly.

Imamu jumped. "When what?"

"When did you deliver the butter?"

"Out to the Maldoon estate?" Imamu asked. Were

they talking about the same thing? To the man's nod, he said, "This morning, sir."

"What!" McDermott's face flushed three shades of bright red. "You went out there this morning?"

"Yes, sir."

"To do what?"

"Deliver butter, sir. I did it before starting time. Didn't you notice? I left earlier than usual." So much for honesty. He dared not tell them that he had gone because he was guilty of not going back to sit with Margaret Maldoon and talk.

Imamu kept reminding himself: I'm almost nineteen. I have to tell the truth for my self-respect. But he had told a half-truth and had to restrain his hands, to keep his fingers from lacing over his stomach.

"Didn't I say not to go out that way again?" McDermott said.

"I did it on my own time, sir," Imamu said.

"Nobody working in this store has time of his own when it's McDermott's orders they're delivering. I'm the one who decides. You went against my wishes!"

"But Amanda said she called you about the butter. Don't you remember? I promised."

"The only promise you make, Jones, is to me. You work for me. I'm the one obedience is owed to—nobody else."

The skin tightened around Imamu's head. His temples throbbed. Anger replaced bewilderment, remorse. Why did this man think he had no honor of his own? McDermott's customers had the right to hold Imamu Jones at his word, as much as they did McDermott. That was the measure of a man. But to sound off like that in front of two cops!

Imamu remembered back to the time when it didn't matter. He would have taken a McDermott on: "Man, you ain't my father," or "My time is the only time," or "If you big enough to sound on me, you man enough to waltz with me." And he'd be ready, or go down trying.

Now here he stood taking a sounding-off from a man who was wrong! First, for siding with Gleaner and talking of replacing him. Then for thinking of and treating him like his "boy"—in front of these serious-looking cops.

Worse, if the cops hadn't been there, still he would have taken it. He wanted—needed—his job. He had to take talk like that because of a paycheck. He had taken a giant step off the streets to be a whipping board for dudes who used paychecks as clubs, to force him to act against himself. How's that for self-respect.

"Jones," the detective said. "What about coming down to headquarters with us. Some questions we'd like to ask."

"You can ask him here," McDermott said. "He's got lots more time to give me before closing."

"I'll come," Imamu said, needing to talk up for himself. Needing, too, space between himself and

McDermott. He had loved the guy so much the day before. Today, he had been prepared to forgive him his changes over Gleaner. Now? He didn't know. Imamu followed the detectives out of the store. Before getting into the car he looked back. Seeing McDermott standing in the doorway, he knew that he'd be very unhappy over the loss of a friend—tomorrow.

The detective who had done most of the talking sat in the back seat with Imamu. As the car sped through traffic Imamu leaned back, his eyes closed. His let-down feeling had to do with caring—and losing. Yesterday, he had been happy. He had had McDermott. Yesterday, he had had Margaret. Today, he no longer knew if he loved McDermott. Today, Margaret Maldoon was dead. Until that moment, he hadn't thought the girl was that important to him. She had made him feel good. The poor rich girl who needed him.

Thinking backward, Imamu felt a sudden horror of his wild ride back into town. He saw himself beneath the tree, with the dead girl. He saw himself bending over to give mouth-to-mouth resuscitation. He wanted to vomit. Never in his life would he forget the heaving inside him as he lowered his face over the strange-looking cold, hard face. Even when he had first touched her, the feel of her arm beneath the sweater had repelled him. He wouldn't even have known it was her—if not for that sweater!

Relieved from a guilt he had not acknowledged, Imamu opened his eyes. Margaret had not gone into the pool because of him! She had not gone in because he had suggested she swim. She had been dressed! He wanted to shout for joy. He wasn't to blame. It had been an accident.

"Could be she went too near the edge and her chair tipped over and rolled down to the pool," Imamu said. "That hill's so steep she couldn't have stopped it."

Their silence forced Imamu to attention. He heard again what he had said. He had talked about the pool. They had never mentioned it.

Imamu closed his eyes and pulled their silence around him. These dudes didn't give one damn about a man's dignity. All they wanted were facts.

He knew the police well. They had taught him. Their being silent was suppose to scare him, keep him squirming. It was. By the time they got him to the precinct, it was supposed to have him dribbling from the mouth. True-confession time. Only he had nothing to confess. But what if he told them he had found the body? They would lock him up—never let him go.

Taking a toothpick from his shirt pocket, Imamu put it into his mouth and closed his eyes again. They might even make a case against him, with McDermott shouting about having forbidden him. And Gleaner? Oh God!

Then they were at the police station. Imamu

walked between the two men through the station and up the stairs to the detectives' quarters. All so familiar. So much of his life's experience. He almost felt comfortable. Almost guilty—except that he knew he wasn't—of anything they decided to accuse him of. A black boy and a dead white girl to them automatically spelled murder. Was it? Imamu looked over the hall which they were passing through. It might have actually been suicide—except that she had expected him to keep his word. Well, cops make their big bills for finding out answers. It was their business.

They pushed through the swinging doors into the office and a voice cried: "That's him! That's the boy who was hanging around the estate yesterday. I told him to leave and not to come back."

James Gleaner walked up to Imamu. He stopped to look him in his eyes. Sullenness like a mask tried to slip down over Imamu's face. He tried to neutralize it. He squared his shoulders, stared hard into the gray eyes: Damn if he'd let this stud talk to him any way he wanted—because he was white, looked like money, and claimed rights to property. That put him on the right side of the law.

"Please, Mr. Gleaner." The plainclothesman sitting at the desk spoke with respect—the kind they gave to guys with the right cut of clothes. "We'll handle him."

So, they had already decided that he needed handling? And Gleaner? What did they know about him

—or the property that he seemed to rule with an iron hand?

"What about you?" The detective spoke to a man sitting beside his desk, swinging a hat between his knees. Giuseppe. "Is this the boy?"

Giuseppe shrugged. "What you want? This boy, he delivers to the house all the time. This morning, I see somebody riding away on a bike. Him?" He shrugged again. "It was early. My eyes, they not so good."

Giuseppe's way of saying friends must stick together? But hadn't Amanda already told the cops he had delivered the butter? Another one gone?

"I tell you I saw him forcing his attention on my niece," Gleaner said. "I warned Mrs. Darcy, my sister-in-law. Now my niece is dead."

So why accuse him? Imamu kept staring at Gleaner. But now the man's eyes shifted away. He turned instead to the detective behind the desk. "I demand that you arrest this boy."

Damn but he was trying hard. Too hard. Imamu took the toothpick from his mouth, to see the man better. He put it back. His niece was dead. He didn't suspect an accident? Suicide? Only murder. He had seen a black boy talking to her.

"Mr. Gleaner," the detective said. "We can't say for sure that a crime has been perpetrated—until the coroner's report."

James Gleaner's eyebrows bristled. He leaned across the desk. Then he looked around agitated, shaking. But he didn't care that much for Margaret. Imamu picked his teeth. Gleaner hardly saw her. He hardly came to the house, except to check up on spending. As far as Gleaner was concerned, Margaret was a burden. So why the act? And why accuse him! What did Gleaner have to hide?

"I hope you're not thinking of letting him walk away," Gleaner said.

"Spillini." The detective who had been in the back of the car with Imamu spoke to the man behind the desk. "This kid knows a lot."

"He was brought in for questioning," Spillini said. "Of course, if Jones has something he wants to tell us?"

It seemed a part of one nightmare—the horror of the woods; the horror of Margaret floating in the pool. But murder! Imamu forced his eyes still, to keep them from turning to Giuseppe. What about Chips? God, how frightened Margaret had been of Chips.

"You haven't given me a reason why you can't hold him," Gleaner said, and Spillini looked worried.

"I know how you feel, Mr. Gleaner," he said. "But it's our job—our duty—to determine what manner of crime has been committed—if a crime has been committed."

"Come on," the detective from the car said. "This kid knows—he knew the girl was down near the pool."

"Oh?" Spillini sat back, staring at Imamu.

"I ain't got no money," Imamu blurted. "If you hold me, I'm gonna need a public defender."

"Public defender?" Spillini said, looking startled. "Didn't you hear? I said no crime was committed. We ain't charging you with nothing—yet."

"I hear. But I want you to know, you don't hold me unless you get me a lawyer."

"That's the trouble with you kids. Too much TV. You get to thinking you're smarter than you are."

"Look," the detective from the car said. "Why don't you come clean and let us decide."

"Not for me, you don't," Imamu said. "A lawyer decides for me."

"Now that sounds like somebody who knows his rights." A gruff voice joined the discussion. "Now who wants to see what kind of lawyer?"

Imamu turned to see a big man dressed in a brown suit with a yellow shirt and flashy tie. Seeing Imamu, the man cried: "No no no! This can't be happening to me. Get this kid outa here. Get him out. This shouldn't even happen to a dog. This has got to be some damn outdated movie. Imamu Jones, what the hell are you doing here?"

Otis Brown! Never in his life had he thought he'd be glad to see Detective Otis Brown. Yet here was Brown, bigger than life—bigger than Imamu had ever seen him—and he was as happy as a just lit cherry bomb on the Fourth of July.

"Know this kid?" Spillini asked.

"Know him!" Brown cried. "Spillini, this kid's the accidental salt in my coffee, the pebble in my sock."

That might be true. The times the two had met, Brown had beaten on Imamu's head, had had him jailed and had followed him for days. Yet each time, Imamu had proven to the big man that he was on the simple side of the law and didn't know a damn thing about order. On the cases in which they had been involved Imamu had been the one to solve them.

"Figgered him for one of them smartass kids," Spillini said. "Ain't charged him with nothing, yet he runs the book under my nose."

"He knows his rights," Brown admitted. "Oughta. He's been a long time learning. In-out-in-out, know what I mean? Jones, what you into this time?"

"Nothing," Imamu said. "This joker"—he jerked his thumb at Gleaner—"been accusing me of some way-out stuff."

"Like what?"

"Mr. Gleaner thinks this boy may have molested —and murdered—his niece," Spillini said.

"Which case?" Brown asked.

"The Maldoon case."

"So it's murder?" Brown asked. "Since when?"

"We ain't got the report in—yet."

"I caught this boy forcing his attention on my niece," Gleaner said.

"And your niece is . . . ?"

"Margaret Maldoon."

"Man." Brown turned to Imamu, smiling. "That's what you go in for now? Attacking rich ofay broads?"

"I deliver groceries out there—for McDermott's," Imamu said. "We—Margaret and me—got to be friends."

"That the same slave you split to Brooklyn to get?"

"Same one."

"And you deliver out to the estate—all the time?"

"Once a week—since the weather's been good."

"So you the boy seen leaving this morning?"

"Guess so," Imamu said. "I delivered butter I didn't yesterday. I had to. But Brown, I want me a lawyer. I ain't holding still for nobody accusing me of nothing."

"You holding this boy for questioning, Spillini?" Brown asked.

"Well—it's your case."

"His case!" James Gleaner said, indignant. "Who decides? How and when did this become your case?"

"One thing sure, you don't." Brown's eyes flipped over Gleaner, taking in the details of his clothes. They were both tall men. Brown much heavier. But one had the look of class, the other of brass. And Brown, conscious that brass was not necessarily heavier, moved cautiously. "But you can rest assured that it's in good hands," he said. "I'm a very thorough man."

Gleaner pulled himself up. "We'll see—who has the final say about that."

His tone, the way he looked at Brown, caused hope to open up in Imamu. Brown didn't take kindly to that kind of treatment. He hated being put down—on anything. Now, his bulldog mouth turned down, his heavy mustache quivered. "You seem sure it's murder," he said to Gleaner. "Do you mind telling me why?"

"I told—"

"I mean outside that rape and murder crap. The coroner's report will tell us that."

Gleaner's nostrils whitened. He drew himself more securely into his elegance. He looked away from Brown to say to Spillini, "If the safety of our citizens rests in such hands, it's no wonder that these people"—he nodded toward Imamu—"take such advantage of the law. Good day sir." He walked out.

Brown pretended he hadn't heard. He looked at Giuseppe. "Who's he?"

"The gardener out at the Maldoon place," Spillini said.

"Got what you need from him?" Brown asked.

"Know what he told me. But we can always pick him up if we need him. He's been working out there for more than forty years."

"Go on home," Brown said.

And when Giuseppe had gone, Imamu asked, "What about me?"

"Got his address?" Brown asked.

"Yeah," Spillini said. "Got it from his boss."

"Okay, kid, you can go," Brown said.

"You got to be kidding," Spillini said. "This kid knows more than he's telling. What if he skips?"

Brown had had enough of being put down. He wasn't having anyone usurp his authority. "Where's the kid got to go?" he asked. "He's supporting his old lady. Did you find out about that before you dragged him in?"

"That ain't part of my job," Spillini said. "Look, Brown, I ain't the one who got off on you."

"Go on home, kid," Brown said to Imamu. "Just you be around if I need you."

"Like you said, Brown," Imamu said. "Where's there to go?" He turned and sauntered out of the precinct.

On the bus going home, Imamu stared out the window thinking about Brown. They had met with the disappearance of Perk Aimsley, then again during the Phantom Mystery investigations, which he and Olivette had set out to solve. They had disliked each other. But despite that, somehow, accumulated meetings had drawn them close, forged a friendship. Brown knew he was no rapist—no killer. If not, he would have had him locked up, for days, without evidence. Cops gave less than a damn about law— except when it involved studs like Gleaner. Dudes with shields against illegal seizure. But he, Imamu Jones, had been working hard to earn that kind of shield. How hard did a dude have to work!

Imamu heard Gail's laughter as he opened the downstairs door. He stood at the foot of the stairs looking up, hesitating. Had she heard about the accident on the evening news? He didn't want to go up and be forced to answer questions to which he had no answers. The day had been hard enough.

Yet her laughter pulled him. He loved its sound. He wanted to be with her. He loved her even when she bugged him. Slowly he walked up the stairs, more tired than he had ever been. He opened the door and when he saw Gail, smart in her tailor-made jeans hugging her slim hips, her white silk blouse draping softly over her bosom, he sighed—softly.

"Imamu," Gail called out to him. "Come and see. Your mother is seeing green—at last. When he went up to her at the window box, she whispered to him: "I think it's a weed but let's make her think it's a plant."

A sudden rage blinded him. Imamu stared at her without seeing her. How dared she! How dared she make his big dream of rehabilitating his mother the stuff of make-believe! Was everything in his life make-believe? He walked away from her, brushed by his mother at the table, went into his room and fell across the bed.

What Gail had whispered, reinforced his growing helplessness: McDermott's attitude with Gleaner; being pulled in by the cops, just like time had stood still. Planting seeds for the perfect flower and getting weeds; discussing plans for the perfect swimmer—who drowns. He wanted to laugh. But it wasn't funny.

Were there people born to fail? People who were meant to dream about, talk about, plan about things that inevitably turned out to be make-believe?

He heard Gail ask his mother, "What's wrong with him?"

And he heard his mother answer, "Something down happen to him—out there." More than her words his mother's tone carried the conviction that whatever happened "out there" was natural to their lives.

Imamu shook in his rage. He hated her! He hated being imprisoned by her limits—the limits of their little apartment. The limits imposed by their past life —and her part in it.

Day before yesterday things had been different—it seemed. Day before yesterday their little place, the window box, were the stuff of dreams—it seemed. He had gone from home, each day, in the glow of achieving, believing his words, his experience, his advice had to count for something—it seemed.

He had encountered James Gleaner, a dude whose eyes had been blackened by fists once upon a time— and suddenly all life was make-believe.

Whispers reached him from the kitchen. Gail giggled. More whispers. More giggles. At him? At his word? At his make-believe-spit-and-paper world?

"Imamu." Gail came to stand in the doorway. "Your mother fixed beef stew for dinner." She waited and when he remained silent, she came to lean over him. "Please, Imamu, whatever's bugging you don't let her eat alone." When he still didn't answer, she sat beside him. "Imamu, what's wrong?"

"Sorry, Gail," he said. "Has nothing to do with— anything." Only it did! It did! It has to do with everything, his mind screamed. It has to do with us. With Moma. With the landlord. With his seven months of striving. Dreaming? He hadn't been making it, but he thought he had. Did his future have to be wrapped up with his past—his life on the streets where he had lived—on the darkest side of the sun?

"Want to talk about it?" Gail asked. Imamu remained still. "Whenever," she said. Assuming, of course, that all thoughts that passed through his mind eventually ended up in her ears.

Ignoring his silence, Gail stretched out beside him. Imamu wanted to move away, but the soft, firm body against his, the silk softness of her bosom, her warm breath on his cheek, forced away his anger. Tenderness replaced it. "In time . . ." he said.

They were close. Since he had gone to live with the Aimsleys, in their brownstone, he and Gail had been close. Gail had always trusted him—her foster brother—just out of jail.

Perk, her little sister, had disappeared. The police had arrested him. Brown had worked him over. Everyone had thought him guilty—his own mother, Ann and Peter Aimsley. All but Gail. Abandoned, he had acted the tough. But never in his life had he been so scared, felt so alone. But Gail—his sister, his friend, the deepest and dearest part of him—had kept the faith.

"In time," he repeated, touching her hair. She moved closer. Their stomachs touched, their breath fanned each other's face. I love her, he thought, in desperation. I don't want to lose her. I never want to lose her.

He thought of Charlotte Darcy . . .

9

Imamu stood waiting outside the gates of the gourmet shop when McDermott rode up the next morning. Pretending his usual affection, he greeted him: "Morning, Mr. McDermott."

"What did you do, laddie? Fly out here to beat the birds?" Same voice, same tone. It seemed that nothing had changed. Despite his simmering anger, Imamu's spirits lifted. "Left my bike yesterday," he explained. "Had to make sure it was still here. And besides . . ." He searched McDermott's face. "Had to catch you in your best mood—sir."

"You did now, did you?" McDermott said, opening up the gates. "Why did you think you needed me in such a good mood?"

Imamu held his answer until the doors were open, until the lights were on. "Mr. McDermott, I know I shouldn't have gone to the estate against your word. I want to explain—"

"I know, I know, laddie," McDermott said, cutting him off. "But it doesn't matter now, does it? Harm's been done." He spoke quietly, gently. But when Imamu picked up an apron from the counter, McDermott's head jerked sharply and Imamu dropped it. "I want you to know, laddie, I've been giving this serious thought. And don't you think it will be best for all concerned—you, me, the shop—if you took some time off? Just until this dirty business is cleared, mind you." The icy hardness in McDermott's eyes shocked Imamu. "A girl is dead, son."

"But Mr. McDermott . . ."

"It would never do for the police to be coming and going in this shop, now, would it? Then there's the idea of having someone—questionable—delivering to my customers . . ."

McDermott kept talking as though he expected a response, even while breaking down any possible argument. However, Imamu could not answer. His breath had stuck in his chest. His nostrils widened with his effort merely to breathe.

What did a guy have to do? He had grinned, nodded, laughed at unfunny jokes. He had worked when he didn't have to. Yet what he had been after all, was an Uncle Tom—a handkerchief head, working for the pat, the smile. The second that image was in

doubt, he was no longer McDermott's good "boy."
The clock had turned back.

"Anyway," McDermott said. "This'll blow over,
lad. On the news last night, they interviewed the
cook Amanda. She said the poor girl committed suicide. Depressed she was, Amanda said. And to be
sure—what with her mother so sick and her so helpless, don't you know? So, it's not as though I'm letting you go. You're still on the payroll—half pay for
doing nothing. That isn't too bad, is it, now? After
you went, as you say, against my word?"

Later, racing his bike through the thickening traffic, sweat running down his face, his neck, sticking
his shirt to his body like a second skin, Imamu admitted that the pain in his chest had to be his heart
breaking. He had loved McDermott. Truly loved
him.

The bicycle decided his course. But had it not, he
would have guided it there. He somehow needed to
be there. He even needed to hear that which he
feared—the squawking birds, feel the chill along his
spine from the hostile woods—now that he had
joined the nightmare.

But when he came to the darkened stretch, the
insects hummed in mild tones, the birds were silent,
and only the darkness of the sunless road touching
his hot, sweaty skin caused the chill he felt.

Riding out of the tunnel of trees into the sunlight,
gazing over the gold-tinged lawn, seeing it spread
out before him, he knew truly why he had come.

The place, its people, had become precious to him. Giuseppe in his gardens, Chips in the background, Amanda, her singsong voice, her ready laughter, her endless complaints, her gossip, her wiles, had made him a part of this household on the other side of the sun. And Margaret Maldoon. How strange to think she no longer waited beneath the old elm tree—for him. How strange that he would never see her again.

Giuseppe, bending over in his garden, never looked up when Imamu pedaled by. No Chips clipped the hedges in the back. And when Amanda opened the door to his ring, she stood eyeing him— with suspicion?

"But what you want here, Imamu Jones? After the things I does hear—and it here you come?"

"What kinds of things, Amanda?" Imamu asked in panic. Nothing she had heard ought to have turned her against him.

"One thing is not to let you in, or around, this place ever again. Gleaner self give the order. Oh, not to worry. I tell him is the police job—to do or not do —not mine. But I ain't feel like crossing words with that man—police neither—after all, he the boss."

"The police?" Imamu said, remembering her betrayal.

"They was all over the place—up to late last night, waiting. What for, I ask you? They can't talk to the mistress. She in a coma."

"Mrs. Darcy?" Imamu's heart jumped, in fright.

"What Miss Darcy? She ain't the mistress here.

Mistress Sophia Maldoon. Can you imagine," Amanda said. "Having one stroke on top of another so, and still here? Thank God she in a coma and can't tell what's happening to her child. It would break her heart. . . ." Amanda's eyes filled with tears. She seemed already to have forgotten that mother and daughter hadn't spoken for seven years. "She about to breathe her last, poor soul, never knowing about Margaret. Oh, Imamu, for the girl to go so. But how? I tell you a hen what covered with dung must a lay she rotten egg on this house. The misery."

"It must be hard on Mrs. Darcy," Imamu said. He wanted to hear about her without asking.

"Darcy? How you mean? And me?" Amanda wiped her eyes. "Ain't it me what look after the child since she born? What with the mother sick, sick, all the time, all the time so. And the child spoiled rotten. Who you think had to care for her? Imamu, you must remember, Charlotte Darcy ain't come back here to live again until *after* the car crash. And by then Margaret was sixteen."

"You told the police it was suicide? It could have been an accident."

"Accident? What accident?" Amanda said. "You don't know, Imamu, that poor girl was unhappy. And she was so low that day you said you were coming and didn't, don't you know? Yes, man. If she went down that hill it was for suicide reason."

"She might have just been trying—maybe to see if she could manage by herself then . . ."

"Might be."

"Then, too, Chips might have tried to take her down, and the wheelchair tipped."

"Who? Chips? But who name Chips?" Amanda asked, frowning. "You know somebody here name Chips?"

"Amanda," Imamu cried, seeing in her heaving bosom a formidable barrier. "You got to know I know Chips. Everybody's got to know that Giuseppe's got a son." Amanda kept staring at Imamu, her hostility deepening. "Amanda. I ain't the enemy. Gleaner's bound to tell the police."

"Gleaner?"

"Yes, Gleaner. Didn't he chase Chips away the other night for peeping in on Margaret?"

Why did Amanda think Chips needed protecting, in such a stupid way, if Margaret had killed herself?

"Gleaner doesn't think it was a suicide, Amanda. An accident either."

"What? He say Chips?"

"Either Chips or me."

"Chips or you?" Amanda seemed to be weighing which one of them she should protect, which one to leave for the bulls. "He can't mean that."

"Amanda," Imamu said. "Margaret told me herself that she was scared of Chips. Terrified, she said."

"Shush." Amanda grabbed Imamu by his arm. "Is that what you telling to the police?"

"I'm not saying nothing to the police," Imamu said. "But why lie to me? I ain't no stranger." She had deepened the wound that McDermott had cut in his heart. He had thought himself making friends, in his new world. Good friends. For the second time in as many days, friends had failed him.

"Imamu, the boy ain't got good sense, but he ain't bother nobody. He been in trouble. Peeping in windows. The boy curious, that's all. He always peeping but he don't touch a soul.

"Is Margaret—sitting around all day, all day so. She imagine all kinds of thing. But before the crash Margaret and Chips was friends. They grow up together. They play together. They love one another. I know. It's me that take care of them both. So why cause poor Chips trouble? It ain't he to profit from Margaret's death."

"Who does profit?" Imamu asked. Amanda gave him a wise sidelong look, then moved away to do her chores.

"And who you think?" She looked around the kitchen as though someone might be listening. "That brother and sister was always . . ." She twisted two fingers together. ". . . so."

"Mrs. Maldoon? Do you think that she'd harm her own daughter?"

"Sophia? No, man. She hate the girl, true. She ain't talk to her since Margaret force the father to take her to Italy for her sweet-sixteen birthday, when he dead in the crash. But Margaret was so spoiled—and he spoiled her. Sophia's a good woman. Sickly—but sweet.

"That James Gleaner, her brother—he's a good-for-nothing. Maldoon make him the executor of the estate—the old man, I mean. And since young Daniel dead, he step in. He the boss. And Sophia trust him. They was orphans, you know. He took care of her all her life.

"He fire the help—the chauffeur, then poor Alphonse, the butler. Things ain't been the same around here since. He tell Sophia the place losing money and she believe him.

"But all that money, Imamu? Millions. He think we ain't know that he taking money out of one pocket to put in the other? And the latest thing I hear—is that a big corporation want to build here. You can see, self. This must be the one place left in the world for thieves to squeeze a city into."

"What's to stop him from selling? If Sophia's in it with him?" Imamu asked.

"The will," Amanda said. "Old Man Maldoon leave everything to his son, Daniel, and the wife, Sophia, but when they die, all goes to the gran—Margaret."

"What about Mrs. Darcy?"

"Oh, she." Amanda waved away the idea. "I got more money from that will than she. The old man leave me ten thousand dollars. He cut her off with one dollar. She ain't count a-tall."

"Then Gleaner can't profit . . ."

"Not if Sophia's dead," Amanda said. "And she good as dead. But leave it to that lawyer. They say he smart as hell. There's a lot to find out around this place, Imamu. So if the police want to know, let them find out, self, nuh? You know how they are? They ain't care one bit about throwing a poor boy like Chips away—to save a man like Gleaner."

"Why didn't you let them find out about the butter themselves, instead of throwing me away—to them?" Imamu knew he sounded bitter.

"Oh, hon, that's not the way it happen a-tall," Amanda said. "The butter was on the windowsill when I get up. The police ask me if I see the body. I tell them I ain't seen nothing. I come out of the house just once—to get the butter from the sill. They ask what the butter was doing there. So I tell them. I tell them Imamu Jones promise to bring it. So I looked to where he might have put it. And there it was. On the windowsill."

Whatever Imamu might have answered, the buzzer over the sink, interrupted. "That's Miss Charlotte wanting her coffee," Amanda said. She picked up the tray. "Nobody in this house sleep last night," she said. "With the mistress getting that stroke on top of the last. It was a hard, hard night." She pushed through the swinging doors.

Imamu waited seconds before he pushed through

too. Going out into the hall, he stood gazing around at the portraits, the bronze busts. He walked across to the living room, up to the window, and pulled back the curtains. As he looked out at the table under the big elm tree, it seemed a long time since he had seen Margaret sitting there alive. Was it only the day before? Crazy.

Would he ever look out of that window again? Would he ever be in the house again? How sad. There would be no portraits to tell of the time that he had been here—no busts, hardly a memory of him who had taken the place to his heart. It gave Imamu a scooped-out feeling. Walking back into the hall, he stood looking at the door of the room near the stairs. Margaret Maldoon's room—on the ground floor because of her wheelchair. He walked toward the room. As he did he felt eyes boring holes through his back.

Ghosts? A house of ghosts. Secrets creaked along the boards beneath the thick carpet. Cries of pain. Pain twisted the faces on the canvases, the sightless eyes of the bronzes.

Imamu neared the door. And a rush of fragrance —Margaret's fragrance—greeted him. He pushed open the door and a warm breeze brushed the back of his neck, caressed his face, moved tiny unknown hairs over his body.

Stepping into the room he closed the door and stood with his back to it. The room was almost bare —a four-poster bed with handrails; a bed table with photographs; a desk with a book open facedown on it.

Imamu walked over to the table and looked down at the photographs: one of Margaret Maldoon—round, chubby, laughter-dimpled face, curly hair blowing in the wind. A happy Margaret Maldoon, the child everyone had to love—and spoil. A picture of Margaret with her parents, Daniel Maldoon—looking more like his sister, Charlotte, than in the painting in the hall—with his wife, Sophia. Imamu studied the face of young Sophia Maldoon. Even then her face bore the look of illness—fragile, too big eyes taking up most of a too thin face, thick curling black hair—Margaret's thick hair, except that Margaret's had been blond.

They seemed the perfect circle of love, and knowing their tragedy, Imamu pushed their happiness from him. He turned away, then turned back. His eyes had brushed by the window and had seen something. A mask? A face? A monster? No, a face distorted by being pressed too hard against the windowpane. Chips! As he recognized the boy, the face disappeared.

Imamu went to the window and, opening it, looked out. No Chips. He ran from the room, out of the house and to the back. No Chips. He rushed to the front and over the lawn where, standing at the top of the slope, he looked around. No Chips.

At the side of the pool, Imamu saw the wheelchair. And it seemed to him that he had seen the chair—without actually seeing it—at the bottom of the pool as he had been pulling the body from the water.

And standing looking down at the chair, hunched over as though it still held a body, he heard again:

I'm lonely, Imamu. . . . Come back—come back—please. I'm so frightened. . . .

And why not? Why wouldn't a helpless, paralyzed girl, unable to defend herself, be terrified at monsters peeping in at her through her bedroom window?

10

Imamu took his bicycle up the stairs. He opened the door and the apartment was dark. He switched on the light and looked for the note on the telephone. No note. The cups from their morning breakfast were still unwashed on the table. Imamu went into her room. Her nightgown lay across her unmade bed.

Had this happened too? Had Moma given in to her old yearning and split? Had she gone back uptown to her old friends? And why not? He had been riding around town, for hours, thinking his own thoughts, suffering his brand of torture. Why did he think that his faith in her would force her to sit forever in a little kitchenette, without a bathroom, waiting while he went out and came in—a simple smile on his face, head up in the clouds—hallucinating. Imamu closed his eyes, reliving his experience in the woods. Nothing was ever what it seemed. He thought of the face in the window—Chips?

He reached in his pocket for a toothpick and the phone rang. He went into the kitchen and answered. "Imamu?" Mrs. Aimsley. "I'm certainly glad you're home. Is your mother there?"

"No."

"Oh, dear. I've been calling all day," she said. "She hasn't answered. I'm worried."

"She's gone." Imamu heard a trace of little-boy hysteria creep into his voice. He bit hard on the toothpick.

"Where to?" Mrs. Aimsley asked. But she knew. Moma had no friends in Brooklyn except the Aimsleys.

"Maybe the police came around—and scare her." Now, why had he said that. An unconscious need for her to know?

"The police? Why the police?"

"Oh, nothing," Imamu said. To assure her? To himself he added, Except that your boy here might be suspected of murder.

"She's probably just out walking," Mrs. Aimsley said. "It's been a lovely day. I'm fixing dinner. Why don't you come over?"

"I'd better wait here," Imamu said. "If she stops there—tell her I'm home, waiting."

"Will do," Mrs. Aimsley promised.

Imamu hung up the phone and went to look out

of the window. It was almost dark. He pictured her outside the window, her face twitching, hands shaking. Where did she go? Uptown? Would he follow?

What if he did and she refused to come home with him? For an instant Imamu imagined her lying on the sidewalk, with him trying to lift her. Her body trapped him—just as he had been trapped in the pool, holding on to Margaret Maldoon's body, unable to let go.

Darkness had completely fallen when the phone rang again. Gail. "Your mother come home yet, Imamu?" she asked.

"No. I have to go get her."

"Where?"

"Where the hell do you think?" What would he ever do if Gail wasn't around for him to sound off on?

"Imamu, she wouldn't," Gail said. "She just went out."

"Since early morning?" Imamu asked. He looked at the cups on the table.

"It's a big city, Imamu. She's been around the house long enough to be stir crazy. She has a right to look this town over. Brooklyn's a big place. She's got lots of seeing to do. Maybe she's lost."

"Gail, the longer I hang around here waiting, the harder it will be to make her come back," Imamu said.

"What if she comes in while you're gone?"

"If she's got a bottle, she ain't coming back," Imamu said bluntly.

"Imamu, where's your faith?"

"All folks that you give a chance to, don't mean you got to have faith in, Gail." Like McDermott, with him.

But Gail—bright college student who thought she understood everything—what did she know about being trapped by the sins of parents. By the poverty of parents?

"Imamu, you sound sick," she said. "I'll be right over."

"Stay out of this, Gail," Imamu said.

"You wait right there." Gail hung up.

Imamu waited. Because she had ordered? Because he needed to see her? Be with her?

Within minutes she knocked at the door. Imamu opened it. Gail walked in talking. "Imamu, you mustn't go uptown. Even if your mother went there, what right have you to follow her?"

"They call it caring, Gail," Imamu said. "So if that's all you came over to say, go the hell on back home."

"Your mother's a grown woman, Imamu." Thank God she ignored his rudeness. "She's got a good mind."

"Winos don't have minds," Imamu snapped. "They have instincts."

He looked into her face and saw all of her: Intelligent eyes, which absorbed his anger, determined mouth, intending to make him listen. He even saw her well-pressed jeans hugging her hips, her breasts pushing up her knitted blouse.

"What if she is there?" Gail said. "What if she doesn't want to come back with you? What will you do? Beat her? Drag her through the streets?" The most important question—Will you stay up there with her?—remained unasked.

Imamu nursed his toothpick in desperation, looking at Gail through narrowed eyes. What if that's where they both belonged—he and his mother. What if their old neighborhood had no intention of giving them up?

"How would you feel if I just left her there and something happened?" Imamu spoke in his little boy's voice.

"Something like what?" Gail asked.

"Death," Imamu whispered.

"Imamu, I know what's wrong. You're upset about the death of that Margaret Maldoon." Imamu stared at Gail, confounded by the haphazard crisscrossing of their thoughts. "That's what was wrong with you last night," she said. "I knew it when I got home and heard about it on television. Today, they had pictures of the house and pool where she was found."

Television! Sweat jumped from Imamu's pores, relief that he had split the scene before the television crew had come. He imagined himself on every TV screen throughout the country. Instant guilt, to a conditioned public. Sometimes even he felt their guilt when pictures of suspected blacks were flashed across the TV screen.

"What's the matter, Imamu? You look nervous. Why? The cook on TV said she thought it was suicide."

"Yeah, I know," Imamu said. But did Amanda really think that? If so, why was she trying so hard to protect Chips? He kept thinking about the monster face at the window. But Amanda had said he had nothing to gain. She had implied Gleaner. So why stick to suicide?

Margaret was feeling low, she had said. And when he hadn't come . . . But Margaret was always feeling low! Didn't Margaret tell him that Eloise had suggested therapy? But then he heard her again: . . . *leave this house. . . . My father was born here! I was born here!* Thank God he hadn't asked what had been on his mind to ask if she wanted to die . . .

"I—I don't think it was suicide, Gail. It might have been an accident, or—"

"Murder?" Gail said. "Stay away from there, Imamu. Don't get involved."

"I am involved."

"You're what?"

"The police took me in for questioning. Her uncle —this big-time lawyer James Gleaner—accused me."

"Oh, Imamu, no," Gail wailed.

"Yes," Imamu said.

"How do you get in such situations?"

"It wasn't easy," Imamu admitted. "My boss told me not to go out there."

"Why?"

"I had a run-in with this Gleaner guy."

"And you went anyway? Why?"

"She asked me to."

"Who asked you?"

"Margaret Maldoon. She needed me."

"She—needed—you?"

"Yeah, we were friends. I promised."

"You go against Mr. McDermott to please a girl? Why? Because she's rich. What did you think to gain?"

Jealous. Gail jealous of Margaret? "Gail, even paralyzed girls need friends. I liked her."

"I'm sure," Gail said. "The princess and the delivery boy. Maybe it was murder, Imamu," she said. "Maybe someone thought that Margaret Maldoon might make you a member of the family—and perish the thought."

Imamu shook his head. In Gail's mind-set, the princess and the delivery boy was even more impossible than the college girl and the delivery boy.

"God," he said, groaning. "Must you sound like them?"

"What do you mean by that?"

"Her uncle accused me of molesting—and maybe even murdering—her."

"Imamu, you know I don't think that. I'd never think a thing like that!"

"If it hadn't been for Otis Brown, I'd have been in jail right now," Imamu said.

"Who?"

"Otis Brown."

"Imamu, this is high comedy," Gail said, laughing. "Thick-skinned Detective Otis Brown—helped you? The next thing you'll be saying is the team of Jones and Brown is at it again." She exposed white teeth in an evil grin. Imamu started. Gail, even without intending to, sometimes had brilliant ideas.

"I don't see why just being accused by this lawyer would have landed you in jail," Gail said.

"I—I let it slip out that I knew where she died."

Laughter fled. Her face tensed. "You did? Why—did—you?" She asked but she didn't want to know. She didn't want to hear. Her frightened eyes begged him not to tell.

So why tell? Who knew that he had been down by the pool? No one. From what he had said, he might have been on the cliff, looking down, and had seen her lying on the grass. Who could prove different? Even as he planned the big lie, the unshakable defense, he heard himself saying: "I found the body, Gail. I pulled Margaret Maldoon out of the pool."

Silence held them. A loud silence in which Imamu imagined he heard Gail's heart beating from across the table. Silence spread—a living thing filling the room, filling their heads, stuffing their ears, until it threatened to crack their eardrums. A knock sounded at the door.

Imamu opened it. His mother walked in. "Sure am glad to be home," she said, looking around the room, and the beat of the kitchen returned to normal. "Guess your'll been wondering what happen to me," she said, sitting down.

She looked from Imamu to Gail, then back to Imamu. "Well, this morning, I taken the garbage out," she said. "And wouldn't you know it? Let the door slam—locked myself out."

"Why didn't you go over to our house?" Gail asked. "Mother's been home. She's been calling you all day."

"Started to," Mrs. Jones said. "But it was such a fine day—and being out of doors, you know? I commenced to walking . . ." She glanced slyly at Imamu. "Thought first, I'd go on uptown to look in on my old buddies. But I had come out without one cent. So I kept on walking. Got to this park, thinking I might just luck up on some of my kind of folks, don't you know?" She apologized for just thinking. "But Son, I ain't met a living soul that I'd take as my kind of folks. So I just kept on walking.

"Got hot. Tired. Sat down. Don't know how long I sat but know I nodded off. And . . ." She looked hard at Imamu, so that he finally asked:

"What Moma?"

"I heard a bird sing. . . ." She said it proudly, her smile broad. "Woke me right up," she said.

"Didn't know what I was listening to. Looked around me. Everything seemed so—like I was dreaming. . . . Then I heard that bird sing again. . . . I looked over at a tree behind me. And there it was—a li'l ole blue bird, sitting on a branch just asinging. . . .

"Then I feel the sun, hot on my shoulders. It felt so good. I heard kids laughing, shouting. Don't know when I heard a li'l kid laugh—

"Been so locked up inside, don't you know. Funny being locked up so deep inside, not feeling even the sun. Inside get to be like a old, dark dungeon, a prison, n'er a spark of light, and knowing that you're stealing away—to your death—and enjoying it . . .

"It's been such a long time since the day I felt your hand on my shoulder, Son. I hung on to it—hard. I had done failed everybody—you, me, even the memory of your father. . . . But you being so good to me, I didn't want to fail you again—so I hung on.

"Lord, I hated you, sometimes. Keeping me from the bottle—my one pleasure. Throat dry, parched—and needing—don't you know. But couldn't get away from the touch of your hand. . . .

"Then today—got locked out and on my own. Lonely. But happy to be where there was no walls. So I walked and got tired, sat down and—then I heard that bird sing. . . ."

11

Imamu turned into the gates of the Maldoon estate, still trying to untangle thoughts woven so tightly together in his mind. It was impossible to see the light. Moma had stepped out of the dungeon of her soul and had heard a bird sing. Time to rejoice. And indeed, yesterday he and Gail had rejoiced, together. He had worked hard for that day. Why had it come on the day that Margaret Maldoon, had been found dead? The day her uncle had accused him? He wanted to cry. One thing he knew, for certain: He had to see this through. Jones and Brown on the case, as Gail had said.

An insistent honking of a horn behind forced Imamu off the narrow concrete road. Gleaner's brown tan-and-brown Mercedes pulled up alongside. "What do you want here, Jones?" Gleaner looked out of the window.

"Meeting Detective Brown here," Imamu said, staring Gleaner in the eyes.

He had called Brown early. Monday morning, Brown should have been in. He hadn't been. The next time Imamu called, he had been told that Brown wouldn't be in until late. He was working on a case. What case except the Maldoon case?

"Brown's office is at the precinct," Gleaner said.

"He asked me to meet him out here," Imamu said.

"Here? Why here?"

"Guess he wants to place me at the scene," Imamu said. "Wants to see firsthand what you accused Margaret and me of putting down."

"Margaret?" James Gleaner's lips thinned. "Don't tell me you were on a first-name basis?"

But the cat had heard Margaret call him Imamu. "I don't take liberties folks don't give," Imamu quipped. And his depression gave way to a savage joy. Gleaner stepped on the gas and roared up the road.

Imamu raced his bike to catch up. The girl dead and instead of being crazy with grief, or acting it, there Gleaner was taking off on him for using her first name. Protecting her? Her virtue? From what? The worms?

The Mercedes was already parked at the side of the house when Imamu rode up. He parked behind it, leaning his bike against the wall. Standing at the foot of the steps, Imamu waited while Charlotte Darcy greeted her brother-in-law.

A quickening inside made him shy. And he was glad he hadn't discussed her with Gail. He liked Charlotte Darcy—the way she looked standing at the top steps, strands of hair, having escaped from the bun, blowing in the breeze. Her lavender dress—the style of the blue she usually wore—rippling around her legs. A poem, Charlotte Darcy—a lovely poem.

"James." She was speaking to Gleaner. "The doctor's with Sophia now."

"Is she conscious?" Gleaner asked.

"No, she's still in a coma."

"I want to talk to the doctor," Gleaner said.

"I'll get him."

"No." Gleaner stopped her from entering the house. "I'll go."

"Do you think it wise?" Charlotte asked, then, seeing Imamu, exclaimed: "Imamu Jones, what are you doing here?"

Her surprise surprised Imamu. He had expected her to show gladness. He wanted to remind her: "you invited me, remember? Anytime, you said." He wanted to share a secret look about the flowers she had asked for—and probably never got. Aloud, he said, "I'm meeting Detective Otis Brown here."

"Detective Otis Brown? Oh, yes, James," she said to the lawyer. "Detective Brown did call. He asked that you wait here for him. He wants to talk to you."

So they'd all be together, talking, fitting together pieces. But he, Imamu Jones, had to get to Brown first. He had the piece that didn't fit.

"What does the doctor say about Sophia?" Gleaner asked.

"She's—hanging on," Charlotte Darcy said. Taking a handkerchief, a lavender one, from her sleeve she touched the tip of her nose. "But I doubt that she'll last the day."

"I want to have her moved to a hospital," Gleaner said.

"Now?" Charlotte Darcy raised an eyebrow. "Why now? What's the use?" She shrugged. "But that has always been up to you, hasn't it?"

They were about to enter the house when Otis Brown's Buick drove up and Brown and Spillini got out.

"Glad to find you here, Gleaner," Brown said, going up to them. "I called your office when I got the coroner's report. They said you were here. There are questions I got to ask."

"Your assistant preceded you." James Gleaner nodded in Imamu's direction.

"My who?" Brown spun around, saw Imamu and stared. Reading the plea in Imamu's eyes, he said. "Jones? Well, he's that kind of kid—know what I mean?"

From the blank look on faces—including Spillini's —it was obvious nobody knew what he meant. Nobody asked.

"Brown," Imamu said, trying to get the detective's attention. "Got to talk to you."

"Later," Brown said, and turned from him.

"No, now Brown," Imamu insisted. But at that moment another car drove up. Reporters got out, then another car followed. From that one, cameramen came out and started readying their equipment.

"Can we talk inside, folks?" Brown's voice said over the shouting reporters. "Just the family," he said, and managed to herd Charlotte Darcy and James Gleaner into the house. Spillini followed. Imamu stood, along with the reporters, staring at the door that had closed him out. How could Brown dismiss him as useless? Wondering what next to do, Imamu started for his bike. But the door opened and Brown shouted: "Hey, Jones, get in here. This talk's for you too."

All the members of the Maldoon household were assembled, fanned out around the large coffee table in the parlor: Charlotte Darcy in the large wing chair at the head of the table. Amanda, Miss Norris, and Giuseppe sat on the couch. James Gleaner in a stuffed chair beside the couch and Imamu in an upright chair near the door.

Brown kept them waiting. He kept walking up and down, up and down, then around the room—a detective out of a movie mystery. Spillini, leaning against the mantelpiece, waiting for Brown to start, kept his mouth twisted—bored with the act. Imamu, for his part, kept trying to capture Brown's attention. Each time the detective looked his way, he jerked his head "get over here." But each time their eyes met, Brown's slipped away, deliberately. Up, down, up, down, he kept the floorshow going, looking first at one, then at another of them until they all squirmed sensing the coming of unpleasant news.

Finally Brown stopped next to Charlotte Darcy. "Mrs. Maldoon," he said.

"Darcy," she corrected him. "Mrs. Charlotte Darcy."

"Oh—then you're not—"

"The mistress of the house? No. Mrs. Maldoon, my sister-in-law upstairs. She's gravely ill."

"I take it you stay here?"

"Yes, I live here. I have for the last seven years."

Sitting in the high-backed chair—framed by it—she looked the lady of the house. Indeed, she reminded Imamu of a portrait.

"I'm a widow," she explained, taking away Brown's need to question her. "My husband has been dead for ten years. I have one daughter—a doctor. So I was free to assume my obligations in this household."

"Which are?"

"Taking care of my disabled niece and her invalid mother."

"Then, Mrs. Darcy, it's my unpleasant duty to inform you that your niece has been murdered." A united gasp, then silence. Imamu sat up, tense. Murder? It was murder? What was he doing here? He stopped breathing, waiting for Brown's next move. They all waited for Brown's next move.

"Murder? What murder?" Amanda said. "I tell you the girl take her own life. She was too down-hearted."

"Margaret Maldoon was hit on the head with a blunt instrument and then pushed in the pool. Death came from drowning. She was unconscious when she hit the water."

"How can you be sure?" Charlotte Darcy asked.

"The blow to her head was severe," Brown answered. "And there was a little water in her lungs."

"The coroner's report?" Gleaner asked.

"Yes, the coroner's report," Brown said.

"Is that all?" James Gleaner asked.

"Got another theory?" Brown looked at the man, waiting.

"I'll have to see that report," Gleaner said.

"Help yourself. Right now, I'm going on that evidence. Margaret Maldoon was crocked on the head —hard—then dumped."

James Gleaner laughed, a short, ugly laugh. "Affirmative action at work? Interesting."

"Look, man," Brown growled, "I been working on the force—"

Charlotte Darcy made a delicate gesture with her hands that bade them stop. "What do you want of us, Detective Brown?" she said.

"Mrs. Darcy, your niece died—was killed—sometime between late Thursday night and early Friday morning. What can you tell me about it? Did you see anyone? Hear anything out of the ordinary during that time—that you can think of? And when she shook her head no, he said, "Can you give me an account of your whereabouts during those hours?"

"Detective Brown, it was a terrible time. My sister-in-law had a stroke. We were all out of our minds —the doctor, the nurse, the cook. I—we—stayed awake throughout the night, expecting her to—to die."

"You all were awake and no one heard anything?" Brown looked around the room.

"No, nothing," Charlotte Darcy answered for them all.

"And you?" Brown said to Gleaner. "Do you live here?"

"No, I don't," Gleaner said.

"But you happened to be here that night, right?"

"No, not at all," James Gleaner said. "I came earlier—then left to go back to my office. I had a disagreement with your—assistant. Then I went to have a talk with his employer, McDermott. From there I went right back to my office. Your boy— Jones—was here when I left."

Imamu looked at Gleaner, surprised. But hadn't Gleaner come back? Hadn't he seen him driving back? Imamu kept silent, trying to think. Why had Gleaner lied?

"All of you were in the house. No one came out to

the lawn?" Brown looked from one of them to another. "No one saw anyone creeping around the place that night? Or early in the morning?"

Imamu looked at Giuseppe, then at Amanda. What had happened, hadn't happened in the morning. It had happened in the evening, or the night. The corpse, when he had touched it, had been cold, hard, as though Margaret Maldoon had been dead forever.

Brown walked up and stood next to Imamu. Imamu's back crawled. Did he want to tell Brown now—ever?

But Brown had walked back down, to stand behind the nurse. "And where were you—Miss Norris, is it?" he asked her.

"With Mrs. Maldoon, sir. I never left her side."

"Not even for a few seconds?"

"No, sir, not from the time she had her last stroke." She stood up. "Even now, I should be with her. The doctor is waiting for me upstairs."

"I didn't say you could go," Big Time Otis Brown said.

"Sir, I told you all I know," Miss Norris said. "I was with Mrs. Maldoon—just as Mrs. Darcy said. Amanda will bear out her story. The mistress took a turn for the worse—about seven, wouldn't you say?" she asked Amanda. Amanda nodded.

"Seven, seven-thirty," Amanda said. "We were all in a state."

"The only stranger about the estate that day, Brown, was your boy," Gleaner said.

"Stranger?" Amanda drew up heaving breasts. "What stranger? Imamu is one of us. How would we eat, if he ain't come all the way from McDermott with food for us?"

"How long have you been working here?" Brown asked.

"Forty years, if you please," Amanda said primly. "I come when I sixteen. I fifty-six now. The only two here in this house before me is Miss Charlotte—and Giuseppe." She pointedly looked past James Gleaner. "It was years before we even hear the name Gleaner."

"Does anyone else work here—besides you three?" Brown asked.

"A woman comes in on Mondays and Wednesdays," Gleaner said. "And—"

"Once upon a time there used to be a butler," Amanda cut in. "And a chauffeur—not to mention a housekeeper."

"But now four live in this house?" Brown said.

"That's right," Amanda said. "Giuseppe lives in his own house, in the back of the garden."

"Why do four people need this much space?" Spillini asked. He looked up at the high ceiling.

"There were five," Brown reminded him.

"Even five," Spillini shook his head.

"Once upon a time," Amanda said, looking down

over her proud chest, "we used to keep every room full—every day in the week."

"There have been a great many changes—as the family gets smaller," Charlotte Darcy said quietly.

"There were four of you that might have been in the yard at the time of the crime."

"You haven't given us an exact time, Detective Brown," Charlotte Darcy said.

"If I could give you the exact time, Mrs. Darcy, then I could name the killer," Brown said. Imamu suppressed a groan: prime-time TV.

"And you." Brown spoke to Giuseppe, who sat twisting his hat between his knees.

"Like I say, I see the colored boy Friday morning —early. Before I start to work. My eyes, they don't see so good."

Imamu moved uneasily. What was that about? Giuseppe pretending to shield him? Why? And why leave room for a change of mind? Just in case? Blackmail. If you don't tell on Chips, I won't tell on you?

Imamu looked around the room. How had they all managed to keep Chips's name out of it? Why?

"Ask your delivery boy about time," James Gleaner said. "He was here Thursday—and on Friday morning. . . ."

Even Gleaner—who hated the boy—was keeping Chips out of it!

"And another thing, Brown," Gleaner said. "With just a bit of probing, I'm sure you'll find that this area was entirely crime-free before McDermott became so liberal in his hiring policies."

Imamu wet suddenly dry lips. He wanted to shout, What about Chips! Margaret was scared as hell of him.

"Don't tell me my work, Gleaner," Brown snapped.

"Wouldn't think of it," Gleaner said. "But if you need me . . ." He stood up.

"Where do you think you're going," Brown snarled. "I'm not done."

"I can't tell you any more than I already have," Gleaner said. "Your boy was making advances to my niece. I saw him. I chased him off. If that isn't motive . . . But then you can say attempted rape can't be proven."

"Who found the girl's body?" Brown said, ignoring Gleaner.

A silence fell. Imamu's ears burned. He tried to answer. He had come to answer that question. But then Charlotte Darcy said: "I did. I went to Margaret's room. She wasn't there. It was too early for her to be out. Amanda hadn't even come out of her room. I went to look for her. She wasn't at the table. I walked over to the gardens. She wasn't there. I went down to the pool, and found her stretched out on the grass near the pool—dead."

"You didn't pull her out of the pool?" Brown asked.

"No. She was lying beside the pool."

"You knew she had drowned?" Brown said.

"Her clothes, her hair were wet," Charlotte Darcy said. "I went—"

"Mother." A voice from the doorway cut her off. Eloise Darcy, in the doorway—a refreshing splash of life in the depressing room—came in and went to kneel beside her mother. "I just heard," she said. "I've been locked away in my lab working, refusing to answer my phone. I would have come sooner . . ."

"Eloise, it's been—horrible." Charlotte Darcy took out her handkerchief to wipe her nose.

"Oh, Mother, what can I say?"

"Nothing, if you're smart," James Gleaner quipped. "It might be held against you."

"Uncle James," Eloise said. "Aunt Sophia—does she know?"

"Your aunt's in a coma." James Gleaner's voice shook with emotion. "She—she had another stroke."

"My God. Because of Margaret?"

"No," Charlotte Darcy answered. "She never knew. She had the stroke in the night—before I found Margaret . . ."

Otis Brown allowed a moment of silence before he asked, "Well, if you didn't pull her out of the pool, Mrs. Darcy—who did?"

Imamu stared at his shoes waiting, praying for another miracle. Brown. Why hadn't he talked to Brown. Brown knew he couldn't commit murder.

Imamu's head hung low, lower. Then, feeling eyes staring, he raised his head. Spillini! Spillini knew! He had run out at the mouth to those cops.

A miracle. God, how he needed a miracle. But no other voice spoke out. Imamu looked up at Brown, who stood next to him studying the faces of the others.

"Brown, it was me. I found the body. I dragged it out of the pool."

"You what!" Imamu's head hung heavy in the silence, burning from Brown's eyes, trying to stare through the top of his head. "I don't think I got that one right, Jones," he said. "Run that by me again."

James Gleaner gave a nasty laugh. "That ought to make things simple for you, Detective Brown. Isn't that what's called an open-and-shut case?"

12

The miracle? Gleaner's laugh? Brown couldn't stand that, especially with Spillini around. Brown liked to be the big show among his fellow officers. That nasty life had to cost Brown a pound of pride.

Once Brown's show had almost cost Imamu his life. When Imamu had been arrested for Perk's disappearance, his life had been in Brown's hands to give or take. And the pride that Brown had taken in that beating had almost taken it. Gleaner's nasty laugh . . . Brown hated folks laughing at him.

"Okay, folks, that all for now," Brown said.

What! Had Brown settled for him? Imamu waited. Chairs moved. Imamu kept his head bowed. He heard feet shuffling out. He stood up. Tense, ready to bolt, he moved to the door, opened it. Outside, reporters crowded around the door, he moved into the crowd, just as a heavy hand came down on his shoulder. Spillini! Imamu jerked away, wormed himself into the crush of reporters. With shoulders bent, head down, he tried to lose his identity. But when he looked up, he found that he was directly behind Brown.

The reporters were mobbing Brown: "What's the verdict, Brown?" "Murder?" "Got the coroner's report, Brown?" During the give-and-take with the reporters Brown kept repeating: "Murder, boys. Young lady's head been bashed in, then she was pushed into the water. Death from drowning."

"Any evidence of rape?" one voice asked.

"Not in the coroner's report," Brown said.

"Any suspect?"

"Not yet, boys. Not yet."

Imamu glanced back. Spillini was being blocked by reporters. Still crouching, he spoke into Brown's ears. "I got to talk to you, Brown."

"Damn right you do," Brown said. "Get into the car."

"Brown," Imamu pleaded. "I got my bike here. I got to get it back to town."

"Jones," Brown growled from the side of his mouth. "Get on that bike and be at my office before I get there. Got it?"

"Got it, Brown. Got it. . . ."

Weak with relief, nevertheless Imamu kept crouched, staying out of Brown's or Spillini's sight. He bent as though tying his shoelaces and, moving around dozens of legs, eased to the other side of the big tree and flattened himself against the massive trunk.

"Hey, where's that kid?" he heard Spillini say, and Brown's answer: "Around."

"What you mean 'around'? I'm taking that punk kid in."

"Get in that car and don't be telling me how to run my case, Spillini," Brown said.

"What's with you?" Spillini said. "I don't get it."

"What kid you talking about?" A strange voice— a reporter?

"You don't have to," Brown answered Spillini. "Just let's get the hell outa here. We got work to do."

The Buick started up. Brown shouted out to the reporters, "Let you guys know when I got something. You know me. . . ." The car raced off.

The miracle had happened!

What now? Get on his bike and go to the precinct? What to say? He had told all he knew, enough for Brown to hold him. What with Spillini foaming at the mouth and Gleaner ready to nail the lid on his coffin. But had he told everything? He hadn't told about Chips!

Why? Imamu leaned his head against the tree and stared, absently into the woods opposite. If not Chips, who? Gleaner? Gleaner was sure anxious to trap him? Why? Not the reason he gave. The real reason. Amanda had tried to tie Gleaner to the crime even before she knew it was a crime! Shielding Chips?

Suddenly Imamu realized he was staring at someone who was staring back—at him? He heard again Margaret's frightened cry: *"Chips!"* A replay of Thursday's scene? It was Chips. The figure moved back into the shadow. Imamu ran.

He ran across the lawn, down the narrow concrete path that the cars of reporters and the camera crews were crowding. He ran through the gates, and from the road, plunged into the woods, then asked himself why he had come.

Trying to adjust his eyes to the sudden night, he heard sounds. Branches hitting against branches, the snapping of twigs. Chips, getting away?

Imamu followed the sounds, deeper into the woods. When they stopped, he stopped, waiting for them to start again. They didn't. The woods were silent. The forest, always so loud with the harangue of squawking birds, busy insects, was silent. He decided to retrace his steps, make it back to the road, then found he had lost all sense of direction. He made his way, in the darkness to which he couldn't accustom his eyes, by holding on to hanging vines and branches, and by feeling along moss-covered trunks of trees. His feet sank into mud, slid on the slime of generations of rotted leaves.

What if instead of going toward the road, he was getting himself lost in these frightening woods? No sooner had that thought occurred, when he found himself blocked by a wall of closely grown pines.

He turned in the other direction. As he did a thundering presence came bearing down on him. A figure loomed before him in the dark. Imamu reached out. He touched flesh—a broad chest, shoulders, an arm. He held on to the arm, which like greased rubber slipped from his grasp. Too late, he remembered Chips's strength. Shoved, his back hit the wall of trees. He bounced back and was reaching out when a blow to his head knocked him to his knees. He jumped to his feet. Another blow to his head knocked him on his back. He sank into the dark softness of rotten leaves.

Half conscious, he lay, trying to feel out Chips's exact position. In his mind, he saw strong arms picking up the wheelchair and flinging it. He saw the chair hit the water and with its occupant sink down, down, down. And in the parlor, they hadn't once mentioned Chips.

The thought brought Imamu to his knees, just as something—a rope? a cord?—was wrapped about his neck. Imamu struggled. The cord tightened. He tried to rise. It tightened still more. God, Chips meant to kill him—and such a short distance from where he had killed the girl!

The boy was crazy. The cord kept tightening, cutting into Imamu's neck. He would be killed out here in these woods and nobody would know. And those who cared . . . ? Funny. Funny as hell. But hadn't he known, from that first day, that these unfriendly woods had it in for him? Imamu slumped against a tree.

The cord loosened. He relaxed. The cord loosened even more. Putting his hand to his neck, Imamu felt the dampness of leaves. His fingers followed the leaves upward. A vine! He snatched it away. It broke. Not even a strong vine. He jumped to his feet, then ducked as something came swinging at him. It grazed his head. He hit out, pushed it away. Sensing it swinging back, he grabbed it. A leafless branch. He pushed the dried branch. It swung back. A swinging damn branch.

Imamu swayed to his feet, listening for the telltale sounds to tell him the direction of Chips's retreating steps. A loud screech made him jump. Then with an awesome suddenness, birds, and insects, started up their clamor.

13

Embarrassed. Brought down in front of a bunch of birds, bees, animals—things like that. Shadowboxing, that's all that was. But Chips had been there. Imamu had heard him, felt him, then he had slipped away.

Imamu trudged up the narrow concrete path. He felt hot, sweaty, and—with his sneakers muddy, dead leaves clinging to his clothes and hair, which he kept brushing away—unnecessary.

He kept on around the curve of the road, then asked himself: So, what if I had caught Chips? What would I have done? Taken him in? Shouted to the police, "He did it, he did it, he did it. I got your man. It wasn't the black boy this time. It was the retarded kid." The thought sent hot blood of shame rushing to Imamu's face.

"I wondered when you would be back." A voice called out as he neared the front of the house. Charlotte Darcy from the table beneath the big elm.

"Who me?" Imamu asked.

"Yes, I supposed you'd be back—for your bicycle," she said. "Although I am amazed that after your admission, you're still free."

"Who me?" Imamu repeated. "Naw. Brown knows I'm no killer. And he's the one in charge."

"So I see," Charlotte Darcy said.

"Yeah, we work together," Imamu said.

"Apparently it's dangerous work." Charlotte Darcy stared at Imamu's head, then let her eyes travel down to his sneakers.

Imamu touched the lump rising on his forehead—put there by a broken tree branch. "Yeah, yeah," he said.

"What do you do for Brown?" she asked.

"We work on cases together," Imamu said. Somehow he was reluctant to tell her what he had already told her daughter, Eloise—that he had been in trouble with the law. "You can say we're sort of partners."

"Partners?" Charlotte Darcy blinked, not understanding.

Imamu, anxious to convince her of his innocence, and that he wasn't just an ordinary delivery boy, said: "Yeah, me and Brown work of lots of cases. That's why he trusts me."

"How interesting," Charlotte Darcy said.

Whether she was or not, she certainly looked interested.

"That's right," Imamu said, bragging. "I'm Brown's eyes and ears." He stopped short of saying brains. That would be a bit much. Besides, he didn't want to hit Brown where Gleaner had kicked him. "We consider ourselves a team."

"Detective Brown—listens to you?"

"He calls me in on his tough cases," Imamu said. "I'm what you might call . . ." He touched the swelling lump on his forehead. "A delivery psychologist."

"Who would have thought you so clever?" she murmured. "You must tell me all about it sometime."

She motioned him to sit and he did—where he usually sat talking to Margaret Maldoon. "There are so many things I don't know about you," she said, and looked into his eyes.

Imamu squirmed, flushed, and stared at his shoes. What if she had received those flowers, which Amanda had taken from him? "Well—we haven't had time to talk," he said. "I'm mostly coming and going."

"We must do something about that," she said. The beat of Imamu's heart doubled. Because of what Charlotte Darcy had said? Or because James Gleaner had suddenly appeared on the steps.

"What?" the man shouted. "You here? Why weren't you arrested?"

"Got any good reason why I should be?" Imamu tried to sound glib.

"We'll see about that," Gleaner said, and walked to his car. He got in and slammed the door, and drove away, the roar of the motor a message of his anger.

It touched them both and they sat quietly listening to the roaring motor growing faint, fainter. "Trouble for Detective Brown," Charlotte Darcy said. "Thankfully the reporters are all gone, or he, and you, might have made the front page—or the evening news."

"Brown can take care of himself," Imamu said. "If he couldn't he would have thrown away his badge—long ago."

Imamu stood up ready to leave. Eloise Darcy came out of the house. "Mother, Aunt Sophia's going to die." She crossed over to stand beside her mother. She shuddered. "It's too much, so soon after Margaret. It's all so horrible."

"Your aunt has remarkable strength," Charlotte Darcy said. "The wonder is that she's still hanging on."

"It is remarkable," Eloise agreed. "Two strokes . . ." She brushed her mother's hair. "Poor dear, it's been hard on you. You have been good to her—to them. I'm afraid I haven't been much help to you, have I?"

"You have your work," Charlotte Darcy said. "That's important."

Imamu started to go, and Eloise, seeing him, said: "Imamu—are you all right?"

"Yeah." Imamu looked himself over for remaining leaves. "I—had a fall," he said.

They were silent, questions hanging all around them. Then Eloise said: "Murder. How could it be?" She looked over the lawn, as though to find some answers there. "I couldn't stand Margaret as a child. Those scenes she used to make, the way Uncle Dan spoiled her. Her demands on him . . .

"But since the accident she had changed. Mother, I wanted to get to know her better. I promised her. You remember, Imamu?" Imamu nodded. "Maybe if I had taken more time right then. If I had stayed with her to talk more about our plans, for swimming . . . Mother, who would want to kill a poor disabled girl?"

Eloise walked around, restless, helpless. "Mother, why wasn't Margaret put into a rehabilitation center? She needed therapy."

"Eloise, you wouldn't have wanted her institutionalized," Charlotte Darcy said. "Taken away from everything she loved? Do you have any idea how sensitive your cousin was?"

"It wouldn't have been as bad as living in this depressing old house, continually sitting under this old tree."

"Depressing?" Charlotte Darcy looked at Eloise, surprised. "Eloise, this is a grand old house."

Imamu agreed. He raised his eyes to look at the

second-floor window, where the curtains hung still. He grieved a silent moment for the woman who lay up there, who had to leave it. He looked at the ivy inching up along the stone walls. It seemed to have grown four inches since the week before.

A grand house. Even the sun had chosen it, had stamped it in gold.

"I hate it," Eloise said. "I've always hated it. The house, its people with all their pretensions. Grandfather—that spiteful old man. God what a horror . . ."

"Eloise!"

"Hateful," Eloise said. "Oh, I suppose he was fond enough of me. But the way he played Margaret and me against each other. He would never let you come to visit. When I came—always alone—he made a point of showing me how fond of Margaret he was. Getting back at you—through me—for marrying Dad. And I knew it. He let me know it."

"That was his way," Charlotte Darcy said.

"Well, his way didn't help Margaret at all. His way is why she ended up in a wheelchair. His way might be the reason she's dead today—the poor, helpless girl. God, no one needs grandfathers—especially rich, evil ones."

"Eloise! I sometimes think you forget that it was he who paid your way through medical school."

Anger simmered between mother and daughter. Eloise started to say something else to her mother, but then she shrugged. Instead she said to Imamu,

"So you found her? How did it happen you came out so early—or that you happened to go down to the pool?"

Imamu thought of telling her his reasons—his anger at her uncle, at McDermott. But how to tell this honest-sounding woman what now seemed to him to be so stupid, so childish. If he hadn't come out that early in the morning, had acted mature, his life might have remained forever the way he wanted it—even.

"She had been a long time dead when I found her," he said. "Her body felt like nothing real. It felt like—like stone."

Tremors shook him, and Imamu wondered if a time would come when he stopped reacting to the touch of that dead body. "She had to have died the night before," he said.

"But Margaret retired early, Imamu. She liked to read before going to sleep. Someone always went with her—to tuck her in—isn't that right, Mother?"

"Ye—es." Charlotte Darcy's voice wavered. Eloise looked at her, sharply. Imamu's scalp tightened.

"You did go in to her, didn't you, Mother?"

"I suppose—Miss Norris—Amanda . . . Eloise, I was with Sophia when she had that stroke. I couldn't think!"

All night? Margaret had been out and no one had gone to look after her—all night! Imamu's mind screamed—along with Margaret's silent scream. He heard the rush of people in the house, people rushing here, there, looking after an old woman who insisted on hanging on—while Margaret was outside being murdered. . . .

14

"Sure took your time getting here," Brown growled when Imamu approached his desk. "I was ready to put an APB out on you."

"Bicycles have a tough time trying to keep up with Buick Roadmasters," Imamu replied. "Besides, I stuck around after you left. I wanted to see what was being put down out there."

Whatever was being put down left a bad taste in the back of Imamu's mouth. A taste he found it hard to swallow. Margaret Maldoon left outside to die while an entire household was caught up—imprisoned—by a stricken woman. A mother who hated her. As if the old woman upstairs had been directing the tragedy. . . . Successfully?

"Your mother ain't dead yet," he had said to Margaret. She still ain't dead. Still hanging on. . . .

"Your sticking around that place is likely to get your butt stuck in you know where. What's with you, Jones? Finding the body, pulling it from the water and keeping it a secret from me? The man who's keeping your butt out of the cooler?"

"Brown, I kept trying to get your attention. You kept ignoring me. Man, you acted as though you couldn't see, couldn't hear, nothing."

"Youngblood, I mean when you were in here yesterday. When I was batting three hundred, in your corner."

"How could I?" Imamu asked. "With that Gleaner standing here, trying to make you—make us—look bad?"

"Yeah, that stud's bad news," Brown admitted. "But you don't be messing around out there, Jones. You got enough possible causes sticking out I can put you in, just on account of."

"Who'd that satisfy but Gleaner? Brown, you know I'm not guilty."

"Don't know no such a thing," Brown growled. "I just ain't rushing in because I've been wrong about you before. Which don't mean I'm right about you now—understand?"

Imamu took a toothpick and stuck it in his mouth. Brown kept frowning at him, then he said: "What else you know about this case that you ain't told me?"

"James Gleaner lied," Imamu said.

"About what?"

"He said he went right into town when he left McDermott. But he went back out to the estate. I saw him heading out that way. I kept trying to think if there was another cutoff route leading back to the city. There ain't."

"But someone called his office about his sister's stroke and he was there."

"Yeah," Imamu said, thinking hard. "Something's funny about that. I aim to find out."

"How's that?" Brown asked.

"I'll stick around out there, listening. There's something about that Gleaner—"

"Jones." Brown pushed his bulldog face across at Imamu. "Don't. You ain't no detective. And you don't have the authority—nor my permission—to go around bugging folks. Got that?"

"Yeah, I got that," Imamu said, disappointed. It would help to have Brown's permission. "But I have a standing invitation out there. I got friends."

"What friends?"

"Amanda, the cook, for one. And Mrs. Darcy. Charlotte Darcy gave me an open-door invite."

"What she want to do that for?" Brown asked, suspicious.

"She can do worse," Imamu said with a mischievous grin.

"Look, lover boy," Brown warned. "Don't be making like a stud for oversexed, aging white broads. They make minced meat of tender young punks like you. Leave this case to Papa Brown, understand? Remember, I can lock you up right now—with good reason."

"Brown, this means my job," Imamu said. "McDermott laid me off. I can't go back until the case is solved."

"Get another slave, Jones. Delivery boy jobs ain't hard to come by. Mine is. And your hanging around that Maldoon place might cost me mine."

Imamu stared at Brown, accusingly. "So what you want from me?" the big man barked. "Gleaner's after my ass. And Spillini's walking around still punchy on account of I ain't hauled you in—yet. So don't push your luck."

Imamu stood looking at Brown push around some papers on his desk. He didn't really need Brown's permission to go out to the Maldoon estate. But his permission sure would make things easier.

The cases he and Brown had worked on together, Imamu had solved. But he had let Brown take the credit. So why act so belligerent? Why refuse him?

Imamu studied the detective. He had never really liked the guy. He had simply grown used to him. He still hated the way Brown's collar went under the fold of his increasingly fat neck. The bulldog jaw, the thick bushy mustache, Imamu now accepted. But his beady eyes still showed Brown's ability to apply brute force instead of intelligence.

Brown looked up, caught Imamu staring, and barked: "Anything else?" Seeing the beady eyes harden, Imamu said quickly. "No, man, no. Everything's cool."

"Don't sneer at luck, Imamu Jones," Gail said when Imamu had explained all. "Brown must have been hard-pressed not to run you in. Look at it yourself. You were on the scene the evening before, then the first thing in the morning. You found Margaret Maldoon's body floating in the pool. You told Brown about it in a room filled with people and here you are to tell me about it. Imamu, your problem is you don't recognize luck."

Imamu and Gail sat on the stoop of her brownstone, whispering. The quiet, the lights from houses around, deepened the darkness. An occasional headlight from a passing car flashed over them to reveal them to each other for brief instants. This heightened their sense of secrecy and Imamu's gratitude that Gail could not see his face, bruised from his bout of shadowboxing.

"The reason he let me go is because he knows he can always find me."

"Give him credit for kindness, Imamu. That's a trait Brown doesn't often show."

"Yeah. He's been wrong so often when he arrests me, it would be damn embarrassing for him to make that mistake again."

"Which brings us no nearer to who done it," Gail said.

"Amanda hints that it might be Gleaner."

"What do you think?"

"I want it to be him. I hate that stud more than he thinks it's possible to hate."

"What about Chips?" Gail asked.

"It's wild, Gail. But in all that question-answer bit, not one person even mentioned his name—not even Gleaner."

"Maybe Gleaner is holding back. If Brown don't pin the murder on you, he's still got Chips. You know, the black delivery boy or the retarded kid."

Even in the darkness Imamu looked away from Gail. He bowed his head, ashamed. Was that why he had gone after Chips? To keep the cops off him? It sure would be easier than to tag Gleaner.

"Could Chips have done it, Imamu?" Gail asked.

Imamu sighed. "I don't know, Gail. He always seemed—the gentle type." He hadn't told Gail about Chips in the woods, or of Margaret's fear of the boy. But her question forced him to face his strange action. "It takes a real violent somebody to beat an invalid over the head."

Imamu remembered Margaret looking up at the sick woman's window. *Will she go and never forgive* . . . But Sophia Maldoon hadn't gone nowhere. She was still there—hanging on.

"It might not have been for profit, Gail," Imamu said. "It might have been for spite."

"Spite?"

Imamu shook his head. He didn't want to say

something crazy. But he had been thinking of some crazy things, since Margaret Maldoon's death.

"I don't know," Gail said. "I believe in looking for the one who has more to gain—when it comes to these millionaires. You said James Gleaner is the executor of the estate?"

"Yes—he pretty much runs things around there."

"Looking after his sister's interest, I suppose. Look, I'll do some research—find out what I can."

"How can that help?"

"You forget, I'm about being a big-time lawyer." Gail laughed. Imamu wanted to answer, but the door opening behind them prevented him.

15

Imamu's first two cases he had worked on foot. This time he had a bicycle. If he kept on with detective work, maybe in fifty years he might work his way up to a car. Imamu liked the joke of it. He might as well joke. What he was about to do was crazy. He intended to get upstairs into Sophia Maldoon's room.

He couldn't ask permission, nor could he simply walk upstairs, knowing that he would be denied on both counts. He had to be sneaky. Sneaking with Amanda, Miss Norris, and Charlotte Darcy, coming in and going out, was no easy trick. But to the drunk, the fool and the lucky, all things were possible.

Wasn't it equally difficult for Sophia Maldoon to pretend sickness with them always around? It was known, sickly folks—especially those who had been sickly all their lives—developed ways of fooling folks, even their own doctors.

Amanda had said brother and sister were close. Were they close enough for the mother to pretend sickness—have folks running around like sheep while murder was being done outside? That's what he, Imamu Jones, detective, intended to find out.

Giuseppe was clipping the back hedges when Imamu rode up. Dismounting, he laid his bike at the side of the road and went over to him. "Hey, Giuseppe," he said. "How ya doing?" Giuseppe looked around, saw Imamu and turned from him. "What's the matter, Giuseppe. What'd I do?"

The old man kept on clipping the hedges. Imamu kept standing. "I got my work," he said to Imamu.

"Giuseppe," Imamu said. "I ain't done nothing. If you thought it was me riding outa here Friday morning, you should have told. I got nothing to hide."

"Got troubles of my own," Giuseppe said. "I don't care for you."

"What troubles? Chips?" Imamu asked.

"Leave my boy outa this." Giuseppe turned on him. "He got nothing to do with you."

"I can't leave him out," Imamu said. "Nobody's being left out—even me. I got to see Chips. I want to find out if he saw Gleaner back here Thursday evening. Did he see Gleaner and Margaret together?"

"Margaret?" The man's shaggy brows shook. "Miss Margaret to you."

"Look, man," Imamu said, angry sweat breaking

out on his face. "I happen to know that Margaret was scared like hell of Chips." He spoke cruelly. He hated that the gardener was trying to make like James Gleaner—on him.

"What you talking about?" Giuseppe asked.

"I'm talking about the police," Imamu said. "I'm talking about them finding out how many times Margaret caught Chips peeping in on her when he was supposed to be out back cutting hedges."

Imamu walked back to his bicycle and, still angry, rode up to the back door. Where the hell did the old fool get that stuff—Miss Margaret . . . ?

Amanda opened the back door to Imamu's ring. She, too, upset Imamu. "Oh, is you," she said. "But you ain't working for McDermott no more. What you want?"

Everybody trying to keep him in his place. Suddenly he was no longer a member of the family. "No," Imamu snapped. "I'm not working for McDermott. I'm working for Detective Otis Brown."

"Eh-eh," Amanda said. "But what he want with you?"

"I been working with him—and the law," Imamu said. "Brown thinks because I'm such a trusted member of the family—I can help him out."

Amanda put her hands on her hips. She looked him up and down. "I'm here to investigate everybody's favorite boy—Chips," he said.

"But how you talk?" she said, her hands going to her heart.

"Amanda, I caught Chips peeping in Margaret's window. I know he always peeped into her window. That's why she was scared."

"Imamu, it ain't that way," Amanda said. "The boy did love Margaret. He feel so sorry for her in that chair, all day, all day so. When they was little she used to beat him up. He let her. They always played so together. Only since the accident. Nightmares, you know. From the father's death she get them."

"Maybe Chips tried to get even—for her beating on him," Imamu said. Amanda looked at him, suspicious.

"You sure Brown got you working with him? He need his head looked after," she said. "Imamu, the boy ain't got the mind what remember those things."

"Why is Gleaner so hard on Chips?" Imamu asked.

"Because Margaret complain so. Oh, I ain't know, Imamu, I think sometimes somebody turn the girl from Chips. Then Chips, too, with his peeping, don't you know."

"Amanda," Imamu said, changing the subject. "Why is it that Mr. Gleaner never put his sister in a hospital? You said she's been sickly."

"Hospital? Where? Those two are close, you know. They were orphans. Poor. And he worked hard, hard, to raise himself, put himself to school, so he could take care of his sister. He don't want her out somewhere where he can't see her when he want."

She took the coffee maker and put it on the table, and as she adjusted the filter she said, "She too. Don't want to leave. She don't want to leave him and she don't want to leave this house, what her husband put her in. Anyhow, where to get better care than what Miss Norris give?

"That poor Miss Norris. She was sitting right here, I tell you. I had just put a bowl of soup in front of her. Then here come Miss Charlotte running—the mistress done had another stroke. What? Miss Norris had been up there with her, until that minute? But what to do?

"God, Imamu, what a night. Is luck we still got we good minds. Upstairs, downstairs . . ."

"Did you actually go upstairs?" Imamu asked.

"To be sure. I went upstairs to the room. And then I went out of the room to call the doctor and Mr. Gleaner."

"But did you see her?" Imamu insisted.

"Who? Sophia? Sure I see her. Looking like she dead. What to do? Miss Norris was doing what she know. Mrs. Darcy was right there, sitting, holding her hand. I had my own work."

"But Gleaner—wasn't he here?"

"No. Gleaner leave before you, that afternoon," Amanda said. Then she looked at him. "But you know, Imamu, come to think of it—I did feel him.

"You know how some people does give out a

strong presence? Gleaner's one. He give out a evil presence. I always know when he's around. And another thing—Chips ain't come around, not even for his food. When that man's about, Chips know and he—vamoose." She picked up the kettle of boiling water and moved from the stove to the table.

"Come to think about it, I ain't seen the boy today. . . . Look how the garbage does pile up. Imamu, darling," she said, shifting to tones of endearment. "Be a sweetheart, nuh? Take out the garbage for me. . . ." And their relationship clicked back to its old footing.

Imamu gathered the garbage in and around the bin, pushed it into a plastic bag. Amanda kept talking.

"You know, that's why I feel surprised to call his office and find him." She poured the hot water into the coffeepot. "Because I feel his presence so strong that night, don't you know."

Imamu, grateful for the chance it gave him, stepped outside to put the garbage in the pail. He then walked to the front of the house and looked up. The curtains of the sickroom were still. He half expected them to move, half expected Charlotte Darcy to look out and smile down at him. What then? Invite him up? Into the sick lady's room? Hardly.

Running up the steps, he pushed at the door. It swung open. He entered the hall and immediately a spirit of adventure took over. So many times he had walked through that hall. This time, it might be called breaking and entering.

Imamu crossed the heavily carpeted floor. Every eye in the portraits stared at him. He walked to the stairs, and the intensity of their stares made every nerve, every muscle along his back, quiver. He concentrated on taking one step at a time, one step at a time. Getting to the landing, he ducked out of their line of vision.

Imamu had imagined he knew the exact location of the sickroom. But the long corridor had many doors. He kept trying to place the room in relation to the entrance, to the stairs. But standing in the hall sweating, heart pounding, his mind a blank, he decided to leave all to adventure—and chance.

Moving quietly down the hall, listening for sounds, human sounds, house sounds, strange sounds, he walked down the corridor remarkable for its absence of sounds and stopped at the first door. He listened. Nothing. He turned the knob. The door opened. The room was empty, its furniture shrouded in white sheets. Closing that door, he moved on to the next.

He pushed open the door and a shower of lavender hit him, caught him in his gut. Surprised, he stood with alarms sounding throughout his body: Thief! Rape! Murder! shouted through to his ears. Get out! Get out! But he could only stand, breathing deeply, the perfume forcing thoughts of blue flirting eyes, flowers . . .

This is not why you came. Not why you're here, Imamu Jones. There's work to be done. Get to it. Easing into the room, he closed the door and stood looking around at bits of clothing—stockings, a blue satin slip, brassieres, a blue satin bikini—scattered around. Imamu tried to imagine his mother in a bikini. Couldn't. But then Charlotte Darcy was a woman forever young. . . .

The queen-size, dark mahogany bed was spread with blue sheets—silk. Bedthings of silk! Paintings—tiny squares of scenery—decorated the walls. Taking up space on an oversize dresser, a photograph stood surrounded by an arrangement of fresh flowers. Imamu moved toward the dresser. As he did a shadowy figure stepped out of a mist and headed for him.

He froze. Licking suddenly dry lips, he took a step back. The figure stopped and also took a backward step, away from him. Imamu sighed, relieved. The tall, slim black dude staring at him through the steamy mirror also wore his hair Afro-style. Then Imamu knew what he had been hearing. A shower. Someone was taking a shower in the adjoining bathroom.

He backed out of the room and stood leaning against the door, his knees weak. He heard the rattle of cups on the stairs. Amanda on her way up with the morning coffee. Imamu panicked. His knees gained instant strength. He ran to the end of the corridor, and stepped into a room.

A mistake! Lights were on in the room. The humidity of a recent shower, of perfume—a man's cologne—hung heavy in the air. On the unmade bed, a suitcase was open. Clothes, a man's—socks, underwear, pajamas that had been used—were strewn over the bed.

He's here! James Gleaner is here—in the house! In this room! The hairs at the back of Imamu's neck curled, moved. He opened the door, but looking out, saw Amanda knocking at Charlotte Darcy's door. He stepped back.

Breaking and entering had to be the weakest case against him. Gleaner could kill him and be in the right! Imamu kept his ear against the door, listening, waiting for the instant to bolt. But waiting, realized the complete silence surrounding him. Moving cautiously, he went to the partially open bathroom and peered through the door.

A comb, brush, toothbrush, and toothpaste were spread out over the marble top of the sink. But Gleaner had been there only seconds before. He had to be near. So Amanda's "feel" of the man was just so much mumbo jumbo.

Going back toward the door, he glanced out the window, and as he saw his bike leaning against the wall near the kitchen, his knees almost gave way.

What if Gleaner had looked out, had seen the bike, and even now was outside looking for him? Imamu's first impulse was to jump out of the window, make it on his bike, flying. But he was afraid of heights. Then, too, he had come expecting adventure.

Man, you're this brave detective. You're here to find clues, trap the culprit. So, what is this crazy weak-knee running you putting down?

Gleaner's here. He's probably in with his sister now. They're probably talking, plotting. . . .

But the spirit of adventure that had spurred him had now deserted him. He tried to revive it but could only muster a vague curiosity. With fear spreading through him, Imamu forced himself to search the desk. Its top was bare; the drawers, empty. No papers? Imamu looked around for a briefcase. None. Did businessmen go around without their briefcases? Papers?

Then he remembered the bits of paper carelessly thrown around the bin in the kitchen that he, Imamu, had put out in the garbage. Among those papers there could be evidence.

An explosion of relief came with his decision that outside in the wide-open-easy-to-run space had to be the best possible place to keep his investigation going.

Opening the door, he peered out. The corridor was empty now. Easing out of the room, he tiptoed down the corridor, using all of his control to keep from flying down the stairs and out of the house.

Slowly, deliberately, Imamu made his way toward the steps. He was almost there when he heard a voice coming from the room he was passing. "So-

phia." Imamu stopped and leaned his ear against the
door. The door swung, noiselessly, open. And there
he stood in the doorway of a large bedroom. It had
its own living room–type furniture—a couch, chairs,
table. The king-size bed was near the wall. And from
the bed, the voice had come—was still coming.

"Please, Sophia . . . We don't have much
time . . ."

James Gleaner sat at the head of the bed, the sick
woman propped up against his chest. His back was
toward Imamu.

Imamu moved forward, unconsciously, drawn as
much by compulsion—the movement inside his head
circling like a clock from the second he had touched
the hard, cold body of Margaret Maldoon—as by his
need to know.

"Hold the pen. Hold the pen, Sophia. I know you
can."

James Gleaner held the fragile-as-death hand of
his sister, and the pen that he kept moving over the
paper. Imamu moved closer, silently, absorbing
tidbits of information as he came: the briefcase beside the bed; the sheaf of papers in Gleaner's hand.
Sophia Maldoon—frail, delicate, barely hanging on.
Sophia Maldoon, barely hanging on to the pen.

How young she looked. Much younger than Charlotte Darcy, this woman who had always been so
sickly. Younger, too, than Amanda, the one who
called her "the old lady." Her face was marked by
the agony of constant illness, hair thick, curly, black

streaked with gray. Eyes large, gray-green, Margaret Maldoon–looking eyes. And those eyes had seen him!

And knowing she had seen him, was looking at him, Imamu pictured himself the way he had to look to her: black intruder, criminal trespasser. A man she had never before seen. But this black brother had the ability to make her brother, James Gleaner, see blood. Imamu saw it all clearly. Still he moved toward them.

Run, run for your life. Run, man, it's your freedom you're messing with. I do, I do, I do want my freedom. No, hell no. I don't belong here. Not in here. No matter what I think, no matter what I thought, this ain't none of my business. This here's white folks' dirty business.

Still he went toward them. Kept going. Then James Gleaner looked around. James Gleaner's eyes held him, stopped him, stopped his breath in his chest. They stared for seconds at each other, and blood reddened Gleaner's eyes. He jumped up. Sophia Maldoon's head fell back, Imamu automatically reached out his hand—then he felt himself being sucked into a nightmare.

And as in nightmares, he lost his will—to move, to run, his ability to think. Confused, paralyzed, he experienced again the powerlessness that he had in the woods, when forces beyond his control took over. And he stood, a trickle of understanding telling him that once again he had become a victim.

Gleaner struck him. Imamu knew it because he fell. He lay at the foot of the sick woman's bed looking up, struggling against the straitjacket of his own terror.

Get up. Get up. Fight. This is a fight, man. You better fight back. Your life's on the line, brother. This sucker's about to do you in. Yes, he is. He sure is.

Fists full of madness rained down on Imamu—his eyes, his head. He crouched, digging his face in the protection of his knees, trying to force anger. He needed a wild anger to deal with the strength of a madman. But he felt no anger. He felt nothing, no pain, no fear, and no anger. Yet he knew what was happening. He felt blows pummeling down over his head, his shoulders.

Then from between his knees he saw Gleaner's foot leave the floor. The man had to be crazy—mad to even think it. He didn't mind getting killed, but he'd be damned if he'd stand still to be kicked.

Imamu leaned over to his knees, then held Gleaner's legs to pull himself to his feet. And as his face came to the older man's shoulders, Gleaner knocked him across the bed, then leaning over, grabbed Imamu's neck, and squeezed, and squeezed.

Imamu's eyes strained out of his head—all the way out. He turned, and found himself staring into gray-green Margaret Maldoon eyes, staring back into his.

16

. . . slime . . . slipping, sinking down, down. Bugs, crawling, biting, snaking through him, his head, his brains. Sucked down, down, into darkness. But hanging on—hanging on, with Sophia Maldoon . . .

"James! James! What is going on? What are you doing!" Only Sophia Maldoon was no longer hanging on. Sophia Maldoon had given in—just as he wanted to give in to the nightmare, the vine around his neck squeezing, squeezing.

"Stop it! Stop it! I say stop it! Do you hear me!"

Slowly, painfully, Imamu heard. Air came seeping back into his lungs. "Are you mad! How did you get here, James? Why didn't I know?"

Stupid questions to ask when he lay dying.

A woman in white came bustling into the room. At the same time, he heard someone calling him.

"Imamu? Imamu Jones? What are you doing in this house?" The woman in white didn't belong to the voice. The voice was that of Charlotte Darcy. Imamu sat up. He tried to stand but sank back down to the bed. Hands helped him, forced him to his feet. He stood wavering.

"What do you think he's doing here!" Gleaner was shouting. "What do you think you're doing when you encourage these animals?" Words, coming from the mouth of an animal. A wild, red-faced animal with bristling hairs, a foaming mouth. "You're lucky you weren't ravaged—that we all weren't killed in our beds."

And the woman in white: "Mrs. Darcy, Mrs. Darcy, Mrs. Maldoon is dead. . . ."

She had given in. Sophia Maldoon had given in. He, Imamu Jones, had seen. He had looked into her eyes and had seen her give in. He, Imamu Jones, had seen Sophia Maldoon die! The image in his head restored Imamu to full consciousness.

He looked at James Gleaner and saw him picking up his scattered papers, stuffing them into his briefcase. Imamu whispered, through his painful throat, "I didn't kill her."

"I'm calling the police," James Gleaner said. "And I'm not talking about Brown. I'm calling the commissioner." Imamu pointed as he saw the evidence going out of the room in Gleaner's briefcase.

"Don't let him get away with those papers,"

Imamu said, pointing to Gleaner. "He did it. He killed Margaret." But Gleaner had already gone.

"He's taking away the evidence," Imamu said, and Charlotte Darcy, taking hold of his arm, guided him to the door.

"Hush," she said.

But then the nurse called, "Oh, Mrs. Darcy. I had only gone a few seconds—to take a bath, to freshen up . . ."

"It only takes a second to die, Miss Norris."

Charlotte Darcy guided Imamu from the room to the stairs, then down the steps. And Imamu, caught in the wonder that he was still alive, took lungfuls of air. It seemed incredible that a moment before he was actually dying, and here he was walking down the steps, growing stronger with each step. Oh, the miracle of life.

Amanda, waited at the foot of the steps, and Charlotte Darcy said to her: "Amanda, Mrs. Maldoon is dead."

"Oh, the poor thing, done gone at last," she said. Then to Imamu: "But Jones, you're a vagabond, yes. I looking all around for you. It's in the parlor that I ask you to get trash—not upstairs. . . ."

And so Amanda had given him a reason for being in the house. She had released him from terror, the nightmare. She had reasserted his innocence. Now he could forgive her telling the police about the butter.

"Amanda," Charlotte Darcy said. "Why didn't

you let me know that Mr. Gleaner had spent the night?"

"But he ain't here," Amanda said.

"Amanda, Mr. Gleaner is here. I saw him."

"Well, I ain't feel him." Amanda spoke in a tone firm with her indisputable logic. "If he here, he came late, after I in bed asleep. His car not out there . . ."

"Find him and tell him to delay Margaret's funeral arrangements. We must make arrangements for the two—now."

Amanda nodded. She stood waiting for Imamu to accompany her. But Charlotte Darcy, keeping a firm grip on his arm, guided him to the front door. Looking back and seeing Amanda staring after them, she said, "And Amanda, you can start preparing the house for the funeral guests."

They walked outside, Charlotte Darcy and Imamu. Then Mrs. Darcy said, "Imamu, that was a silly thing to do—wandering around a private home. You know Mr. Gleaner won't let this pass."

Amanda had already given him an excuse. "I wasn't breaking and entering, nothing like that," Imamu said. "I was helping Amanda."

"In Mrs. Maldoon's bedroom?" Charlotte Darcy raised her eyebrows to widen eyes as blue as the satin bikini in her bedroom. And as though she was looking right into his mind, Charlotte Darcy smiled. "Looking for clues, I presume, Mr. Holmes. My but you are thorough. What kind of clues were you looking for in Mrs. Maldoon's room?"

"I found it," Imamu said. "I saw Gleaner forcing Mrs. Maldoon to sign papers."

"But Mrs. Maldoon is dead," Charlotte Darcy said, a thoughtful look on her face.

She, too, was giving him an out. If Sophia Maldoon was already dead, it'd be clear that his presence in her room had nothing to do with her death.

It wasn't an out he was willing to take. He shook his head. "Not at first, she wasn't. She was alive."

"Alive and awake?"

"Yes," Imamu said. "She looked at me. She saw me."

"And you saw her sign the papers?"

"No," he said. "She didn't." He recalled the scene between brother and sister. He remembered looking into the big gray-green Margaret-looking eyes. "He was guiding her hand. But then I came in," Imamu said.

"You're lucky I heard the commotion," Charlotte Darcy said. Her smile forged a complicity between them. "I might have been in another part of the house. Imamu, it took courage to charge into the lion's den knowing how Mr. Gleaner feels toward you."

Imamu shook his head and sighed. A lion's den. He felt the punishment of Gleaner's angry fists. "Guess you saved my life," he admitted.

"Mr. Gleaner has a terrible temper." Charlotte Darcy laughed. "Those of us who have seen it think him a monster. He's terrifying. Thursday evening, I saw him chasing poor Chips across the lawn. I haven't seen the poor boy since."

"Thursday?" Excitement closed Imamu's aching throat so that he whispered. "What time was that?"

"I don't know exactly. Quite some time after you left."

"Where was Margaret then?"

"I don't know. I suppose in her usual place. I looked out of the window, and thought of going out —but then it happened."

"What happened?"

"Mrs. Maldoon had her seizure. . . ."

"You're sure you saw him—on Thursday evening —after I left?"

"I'm sure."

"Will you testify to that?" Imamu asked.

"Testify? Why should I have to? Mr. Gleaner's in charge here. Anyone who goes against his wishes will have to tolerate his wrath."

Imamu looked away. He hated thinking of Charlotte Darcy being forced. But he had to tell Brown. His freedom might depend on it—his job, his feeling about himself, all depended on her telling.

And as he chose his words carefully to tell her what her testimony might mean, he heard her say: "Now who in the world . . . ?"

Imamu followed the direction of her eyes, and saw

someone cycling up the path, ponytail flapping, smooth brown knees shining. Gail! What did she want here!

He and Charlotte Darcy waited in silence as Gail pumped up the hill, disappeared around the curve, then reappeared on the path coming toward them "Hey, Imamu," Gail smiled a wide you-can't-get-away smile as she rode up. "Called you early this morning but you had already gone. I got worried."

"What did you think might happen to me?" Imamu said. He had never wanted Gail and Charlotte Darcy to meet. Now he tried to hide his resentment. "I can look after myself." Beneath her probing gaze, his head throbbed.

"Sure looks like it," Gail said, then explained: "Nobody seemed to know where you were, Imamu. I went by McDermott's. He told me you were—off. . . ." She said it in a sly, we-won't-tell way. "Then I called Brown. He wasn't in. The guys at the precinct hadn't seen you. So I supposed you were—on the case." She grinned mischievously. "I took the chance."

"And here he is," Charlotte Darcy said. "Safe and sound."

"Anyway, he's still alive," Gail said, gazing at Imamu's face in wide-eyed concern. She put her bike down at the side of the road, walked up to Imamu to examine him closely, then hooked his arm protectively.

Embarrassed, Imamu tried to ease his arm away.

Gail tightened her hold. "My sister," Imamu explained.

"A lovely sister," Mrs. Darcy said. "You never mentioned her."

"Foster sister," Imamu said, his ears burning. "Gail, meet Mrs. Charlotte Darcy."

"Mrs. Charlotte Maldoon Darcy?" Gail said. Then, to the older woman's nod, added, "It's a real honor. I've been hearing about you and your family all my life."

"Really?" Charlotte Darcy said, smiling.

"My mother's teacher used to bring her out here and so did mine. I've been here before."

"Ahh," Charlotte Darcy said, her face relaxing. "I remember those class visits. The original house was one of the first to be built in Brooklyn."

"I know the bio," Gail said. "It's a historical landmark."

Charlotte Darcy pushed the door wider, giving a better view of the hall. "It would have been a pleasure showing you around," she said. "But my sister-in-law has just died."

"I'm so sorry," Gail said, pushing her way in anyway.

"The doctor should be coming soon." Charlotte Darcy protested, but she seemed unable to resist following Gail inside.

Imamu waited outside. He was angry that Gail had come. He was anxious to be gone. He wanted Brown to know about Gleaner's being there Thursday. Amanda had said she felt him. She just hadn't seen the car. But—a wild excitement shook Imamu. Gleaner was in the house and his car wasn't parked here.

". . . another calmer time," he heard Charlotte Darcy apologize in the hall, and he heard Gail say:

"I don't remember the house being this far out. But I guess it must have always been. Cut away—a sort of kingdom apart, isn't it?"

"Yes, it has always been," Charlotte Darcy replied. "I can remember my grandmother, and my mother, reigning—like queens." Her voice tilted with pride. "Once, European royalty, diplomats, were our weekend guests. My father—great men— walked up and down this lane."

They had come back out to the steps. Charlotte Darcy gestured to the great expanse of lawn. "Here there were all trees. Beneath the trees were benches. Adults used to stroll through the trees, or they sat beneath them talking—romancing . . ." She motioned to the end of the lawn. "Trees grew right down to the dell. We children used to play down there. We used to swing—high, high, in the air— while voices of grown-ups, their laughter, floated down to us. . . ."

As she spoke Imamu had visions of little children swinging, their little legs stretched out. He heard young voices, strong laughter floating up from the bottom of the dell, reaching them on the steps where they were standing.

"We'd stay down until dark, or until Father came to fetch us. . . ." Warmth crept into Charlotte's voice, a fondness for her father, for the times that had been.

"Down there?" Gail said, pointing in the direction Charlotte Darcy had indicated. "Isn't that where the pool is?" A sudden silence.

And Charlotte Darcy returned to her normal voice and said: "Yes, that's where the pool is. Since that time, the trees have been felled—cleared, as they say. Now going down to the dell—is going for a swim. . . ."

They were silent, Imamu and Gail, as they rode through the wooded stretch of road, on their way home. "This has to be the spookiest spot on earth."

"Until you get to know it," Imamu said, wondering at his lost fear of the once dreaded woods. "But I'll say one thing. Man can't understand himself unless he can understand the forests."

"What about women?" Gail asked.

"Gail, you know what I mean. People—human beings."

"Imamu, I do think you are *trying* to become philosophical."

For a moment Imamu thought of explaining. But he didn't want Gail teasing him about a moving, private experience, so he said: "Anyway, once you get through this part, the house and land are worth the entire trip."

"You've got to be joking," Gail said. "Tell me one thing about the place you find interesting. That miserable museum piece. If these woods weren't enough to scare schools from discontinuing those gruesome trips, that old house is. It's really too much."

Imamu didn't believe her. Gail sounded jealous. Of the house? Of Charlotte Darcy? No two people could look at the same place and see it that differently. But to oppose Gail was to fight to the end. He wasn't in a fighting mood. "When does a house get too much?" he asked.

"When it's like that," Gail said. "That house needs maids, butlers, things like that."

"Gail, come off it—" Imamu braked his bicycle and backpedaled. Dismounting, he went to examine the brush at the roadside. Strange how familiar the road had become. A little disruption of its sameness caught his attention.

The brush had been trampled. Following the path of broken branches brought Imamu within yards of a car parked among a cluster of spruce trees. The tan-and-brown Mercedes, of course.

He remained silent as they rode on. But Gail, unable to stifle her curiosity, asked: "What did you see back there?"

"That Gleaner," Imamu said. "He can do some way out things for a guy supposed to be in control."

"Gleaner?" Gail said. "Oh, Gleaner. Yes, I've been checking him out."

"You have?"

"Yeah, early this morning, I was into research. But it'll wait until we get home."

Research? Did she find out all about the dude, in that short time? He wanted to dispute her. But then these college types . . . So he said, instead, "Gail, if a dude offered to buy you a pad like that you'd jump all over my head to grab at the chance."

"A pad like what?"

"Like that old miserable house. Like this big estate."

"Jump over your head?" Gail said. "Why should a sister have to jump over the head of her brother to grab a dude?" Then, on a more serious note, she said: "Imamu, even if I met a guy who confused a relationship every time another woman was around, I still couldn't go for that place. What does one do in it?"

"Reign, like royalty," Imamu said.

"That's not my style. I live the kind of life I like, in the kind of house I adore. It suits me. I could never trade it for a museum."

"I don't believe you," Imamu said. "What good is all your studying if you can't have a dream big enough to make studying worthwhile?"

"My studying is not about dreaming," Gail said.

"Why bug me with school, if I can't have something to look forward to?" Imamu asked.

"I thought you had all that together by now," Gail answered. "What does education have to do with owning a mansion?"

"Look, Gail, if I spent all my life in school, it would be to live as well as the best folks live—or what's the use?"

They had come out into daylight. The heat on their backs relaxed them and they rode almost leisurely.

"Imamu," Gail said. "I live with the best folks. In the kind of place I dig. I love my house. It suits me. It suits my family. When I leave them, I'll be looking for one like it. Comfortable. If I'm alone, I'd want a smaller house. If I have a family, one like ours will do just fine.

"I'm not getting educated to tie myself to impossible dreams. I'm getting educated to know all that is humanly possible to know. I want to understand where I stand, as Tolstoy says, in the scheme of things. I want to be a part of change—for the better of people. Having a big house isn't where it's at, Imamu. Big houses don't free people to work for others. It imprisons them, making it impossible."

"Gail, you talk because you like to hear yourself," Imamu accused. "What's the good of knowing things if you're out of work? I never had nothing. If I put time in educating myself, it's to get rich. I want to be rich. I don't want my mother ever to need again. I want to be so rich that if I throw money away, it's because I forgot I had it. I'll just pull out some more."

"A moment before, you were being philosophical," Gail said. "Now you are talking about the dream of fools."

"That's because I'm not educated like you, Gail," Imamu said.

"That's true," Gail agreed. "To the uneducated, philosophy comes and goes. To those who study, it becomes ingrained. Imamu, nobody goes from having nothing to having everything—unless they're willing to do something illegal, indecent, or crazy. Do you think that's what your mother wants? A big house? Folks in big houses like that never take in foster kids."

"That's a low blow, Gail."

"But true. Can you imagine foster kids playing over the Maldoon lawn? Strain your simple mind, Imamu. They are supposed to be above such things. . . .

"Did you hear Charlotte Darcy?" Gail scoffed. "Looking at all that unused space, talking of bygone days. As they die! Her sister-in-law, upstairs, dead—and she's downstairs getting kicks, talking about ghosts. Her niece is dead. Mrs. Maldoon is dead. And Charlotte Darcy is dying. She's a dying breed—and who cares!"

"So," Imamu said, still stung by Gail's words. "Mrs. Aimsley took in a foster child."

"Yes," Gail said. "Because loving folks and caring about them counts, Imamu Jones. That's what's got to count. After that, having is just for the sake of having. And that's sick."

Gail had offended him. She wanted to. She thought by being blunt she could force him to see all things the way she did. "Mother cares about foster kids," she said. "She cares about all kids. She's a friend, and a damn good one, Brother dearest. I like it that way."

"You talk like that because you always had, Gail."

And that had to be it. That had to be the reason they looked at the same things and saw them completely differently. Gail belonged to those who had never really needed. Hers was a breed satisfied to look good, to live well, eat things for kicks. She loved her parents, liked the way they lived, and that was the way she wanted it.

Imamu understood the guys—out there. Street dudes. He understood their dreams. Big dreams, blown up in their minds behind their eyes: A car— but a Cadillac. A house—but a mansion. Clothes— but far-out, expensive cuts. Dudes overlooked from birth. To other folks one of those dudes was like a replica of the other. Which made their needs even bigger than their big dreams.

"I never had anything, Gail," Imamu said. "But we live in a country where to dream is to have. I want to have it all—big house, land, the works. I don't mind working hard for it. But I intend to get it."

17

Imamu was still upset with Gail when they arrived at the precinct. Gail, her mind forever churning, working up arguments to win over Imamu. She walked up to Brown's desk.

"Remember me?" she asked.

"Hey, you're the Aimsley kid," Brown said. "How can I forget you? You look great. A bit more —but so much the better—know what I mean?"

"So you and Imamu are working on the Maldoon case together," she said.

"Who put that lie out?" Brown cut his eyes over to Imamu, sprawled in the chair next to the desk. Then he did a double take. "Imamu Jones, looks like you been putting your eye in the wrong keyhole again."

"We just come from the Maldoon place," Imamu said.

"So, Gleaner got hold of you?" Brown guessed. "Told you to keep away."

"Can't, Brown. There's things we got to know. Things I can get to quicker than you."

"So I see," Brown said, nodding his head, at the swelling over Imamu's face. "And you brought your girl along—to meet the family? Things getting serious, huh, Jones?"

"Quit kidding," Imamu said.

"And what's with that voice?" Brown looked at Imamu, studying him hard—his throat, his swollen face. "That's called learning the hard way, Jones."

"Brown," Imamu said, ignoring the man's jabs. "Gleaner did go back to the place Thursday—after he left McDermott. Mrs. Darcy saw him."

"How come she ain't said so before?" Brown asked.

"Guess she ain't thought it important," Imamu said.

"Man, you got to be kidding," Brown said. "Seeing the dude, near the scene of the murder?"

"She still don't think it's that important. And I didn't let on to her how important I thought it was."

"Imamu Jones, the woman's grown—and I suppose intelligent."

She hadn't told because of Chips. Poor, simple Chips, whom everyone has to keep secret—from Gleaner, from Brown. A big, six-foot-two secret. And yet he, too, kept from talking to Brown about the kid. He didn't want to think of Chips in Brown's strong, persuasive hands.

"The old lady's dead," Imamu said. Then, thinking of how young Sophia Maldoon actually appeared, he added: "Mrs. Maldoon. And Brown, I saw Gleaner trying to force her to sign something—a will, I think."

"You sure do get into—things, Jones. How come you seen that?"

"I—I—was there. Anyway, I don't think she signed it. She was too weak."

"She was supposed to be in a coma?" Brown said.

"Not just before she died," Imamu answered. "She looked at me, Brown. Her eyes saw me."

"Even women in comas see when you're around. How do you do it, Imamu?"

"It must be his charisma," Gail said. "You ought to see the way Charlotte Darcy looked at him!"

"Why did Gleaner wait so long to draw up a will?" Brown asked, speaking more to himself than to Imamu. "He knew the old girl was sick—had been sick. Sick people sometimes die—especially from heart attacks, strokes, stuff like that."

"It wasn't a will," Gail said. "Neither he nor his sister can abrogate the will of the senior Daniel Maldoon."

"What do you know about it?" Brown asked.

"I did some checking today," Gail said.

"Well now, not only do you look grown, you sound like my kind of woman."

"What did you find out?" Imamu asked.

"That the senior Daniel Maldoon made his lawyer, the brilliant James Gleaner, the trustee of his estate, until—or in case—something happened to his son, and his wife. Then the estate is passed down to his grandchildren."

"So?" Imamu asked.

"So whatever you saw him trying to make her sign, it wouldn't be a will."

"Then what would be so important?" Imamu asked, and Brown answered:

"That's what we gotta find out, Jones."

Imamu stood up, disappointed. He didn't accept Gail's explanation. She had said that to discredit him. She had been trying to discredit him a lot lately.

"Look, Brown." He stood up ready to leave. "I came to report that Charlotte Darcy seen Gleaner on Thursday. That's not all. We just seen Gleaner's car parked on the road in the woods where nobody's likely to see it. Which means he could come, do his dirty work, and go with nobody seeing him."

Imamu thought of telling Brown about Amanda "feeling" Gleaner that night. But remembering his morning experience, he didn't. He kept silent about Chips too. Now he knew why Chips was lying low, hiding. Chips had seen Gleaner's car, knew that he had been around. . . . Chips had probably seen lots more.

"Right side or left side of the road?" Brown asked.

"Right side coming, left side going," Imamu said.

"Good work, Jones. Those are the little things that might eventually lead to the answer."

"Gonna take Gleaner in?" Imamu asked.

"On what charge?" Brown asked. "We got enough to ask him some tough questions—but we got to keep digging."

18

"So, you're up to your neck in murder, Mr. Hercule Poirot," Gail said.

"All the way," Imamu answered. "There's only one way to be a great detective, baby. That's to work at it. Why do you think Brown spared me? He wanted me to be out here—to get the thing done, Gail. I ain't no ordinary cat."

"With your hoarse voice, your knotted head and black eyes, I can see you're no ordinary cat—more like an alley cat."

Imamu shook his head. He refused to be drawn into a quarrel. "If I studied philosophy or psychology, I'd be just about the baddest detective around. Did you know, Gail, I can look at folks' heads and see right into their minds?"

"God preserve us from grocery boys and dime store detectives," Gail groaned.

Imamu bit his lips; she was getting him angry. But he joked: "Might even get to be the black Philip Marlowe—with a bit more class. Don't need much education for that, right?"

"Have you stopped to think, Imamu, even school dropouts in jail sometimes study to get somewhere?"

"You forgive me for saying to Mrs. Darcy that you were my sister?" Imamu said, teasing.

"Imamu, since when does one and one add up to five?" Gail asked. "That's what's wrong with school dropouts. Always using figures wrong."

"The figures might be wrong, but what'll you bet I come up with the proof to jail Gleaner—for life."

"Imamu, you need more than good looks to become a private detective."

"Well, it doesn't hurt," he said. "I'm even with you. You did all that research and you come up with what I've been knowing. That Gleaner's the executor of the estate."

"Trustee," Gail said, correcting him.

"Trustee then." Imamu shrugged. "Whatever you want to call him, I'm gonna be the one that's gonna nail him."

"Oh, please, Imamu."

"Bet me, bet me."

"Bet. So when are we going back?"

"Back where?" he asked.

"To the Maldoon place."

"We?"

Gail smiled a bright trying-to-look-more-intelligent smile. "You don't think I'm going to let you have all the fun, do you?"

"Fun! What fun?" Anger, which he had been holding back, rose. "Gail, a girl's been killed, murdered. Does that sound like fun?"

He wanted to add that he had almost been killed. That he was tired, sick, sore and needed a rest. What he didn't need was a clean-living, unsoiled—spoiled—chick to give him lessons on where he had come from, what he had been, what he now was or what he might be ninety years from now.

"Imamu, you know I didn't mean fun fun. I mean interesting."

"Your breed of people, Gail, can't tell the difference between what's fun and what's interesting."

Imamu was surprised at how near he was to the breaking point. Surprised, too, by the pain caused by Gail's careless remark. It pointed up his total involvement, his step-by-step anguish: first finding and touching the dead girl's body; then his strange mind-opening experience in the woods. And today he had looked into the eyes of a woman, had seen her die while her brother was trying to choke him to death.

Every one of the happenings had marked him—real deep. Yet here he was trying to act like the old Imamu Jones. But one more insult from Gail Aimsley's lips and he would have had it.

"Look, Gail," he said, looking up at the door of the brownstone. He spoke softly, carefully, knowing how near his anger was to breaking out . . . Tomorrow, the day after, he might feel different, might even feel all of his tenderness toward Gail. But now . . . "I don't know what I'll be doing. I want to help out Brown. And I have things to do—to talk about with—some folks."

"With Charlotte Darcy," Gail said accusingly.

"Her too. And I don't want you around."

"It seems to me, Imamu Jones, that if you have anything to talk over with Charlotte Darcy, you'll be needing me around."

"Jealous?" Imamu hid his irritation in a laugh.

"Jealous?" Gail said. "Why do I have to be jealous of that old lady?"

"Older woman!" Imamu said, correcting her. "Older—and beautiful. . . ."

"Beautiful! Oh, come off it, Imamu. Because Charlotte Darcy's got blond hair—and blue eyes?"

"Because she's got class," Imamu said.

"Is that what you call it, class? How very ordinary. A big house and nostalgia—you call class?"

"Wow," Imamu said. "The way you take on a rival."

"And have you looked into her eyes?" Gail's eyes were darkened by anger. The whites of them flashed a bright white. "I mean have you really looked?" Imamu controlled his hand to keep from reaching into his pocket for a toothpick. What if he told her how deeply he had looked?

"Expressive," he said.

"Because they're blue?"

"No, because . . ." He wanted to say because they held secrets—very personal secrets between them. "They're penetrating," he said. "They read people."

"Balls," Gail said. She picked up her bike and walked up the steps of her stoop.

"What does that mean?" Imamu asked.

"And bats," Gail called without looking back. "Vampires . . ."

19

Twelve days. Twelve days since he had pulled Margaret Maldoon's body from the pool. Eight days since he had seen Sophia Maldoon die. Four days since he and Moma had seen James Gleaner being arrested, at the funeral, as they watched on the TV set. Since then Imamu had been waiting—forced to wait—on this side of the sun.

Not wanting Moma to know he wasn't working, he walked the streets, sitting in the park instead of at home. But now—now he was finished waiting.

"Thought I'd let you sleep," his mother said when he came into the kitchen. "The way you were snoring, I figured you was tired."

He was tired. Tired, lonely, bored, and feeling left out of everything.

Imamu had called Amanda the day she was leaving for the double funeral. She had promised to call back. She hadn't. He had called again after Gleaner's arrest, wanting to talk to Mrs. Darcy. The telephone rang and rang. No one had answered.

Finally, Imamu had left the household to its grief. Since then restlessness claimed him. He went to sleep only to court nightmares. He called Brown. He was never in. Not knowing what was happening was driving him mad. He had to find out.

Nor was it mere curiosity. He was involved, damn it. Deeply. More, he was disturbed by something—something he knew? Something he had heard? Something he hadn't hooked up—something right at the tip of his mind.

"See you, Moma," he said, going for his bike.

"Ain't you gonna have tea?"

"No, I'm late. Got to go."

He looked away from her worn face, her small, used-up body. The sight of her sent dreariness through him—a depression. He had pulled her back from the dead, put her into this dreary apartment. Now he was dying and she couldn't help him. She had no spark to drive him. He had made her live—now she had nothing to offer.

Nor did he have more to give to her. They had nothing to give to each other. The weight of another day, of another night, when he came in or went out, when he slept, overwhelmed him. He hated the thought of being with her.

"Got something to show you, son," she said.

"Later Moma, can't stop now."

He wanted to talk to Brown and he was tired of calling and leaving word. Today instead of calling he went to the station. He went upstairs to Detectives, and up to Brown. But stopped before he came to the desk. Gail was sitting there. Imamu looked from Gail to Brown. What kind of conspiracy where they cooking up—against him?

"Hey, man," he said to Brown, ignoring Gail. "I been waiting for your call."

"What call, man?" Brown asked.

"To be a witness, Brown. Against Gleaner," Imamu said. He didn't care about Brown's taking the credit. He knew Brown thought himself too big-time to share honors with an eighteen-year-old from the streets.

"Jones," Brown said. "I got a case to pull together, man. I ain't got time for diddling around." He shuffled papers on his desk.

"What more you need, Brown?" Imamu asked. "We got the facts . . ."

"Jones, I hate to tell you this," Brown said. "But that's why I'm the detective and you the delivery boy. There is such a thing as evidence, dig? And I'm the one that's got to get it."

"I gave you evidence," Imamu said.

"That's it, Jones. *That is it.* When I want to ask you something, I'll call."

"Look Brown," Imamu protested. "I know you got Gleaner. I saw when you picked him up."

"Imamu," Gail put in. "Why should Gleaner want to kill Margaret?"

"That's right, Jones," Brown said. "Your girl here came up with some very interesting reasoning. She's a bright kid."

Imamu turned from Gail, looking smart in a bright yellow suit, to Brown, dressed in his usual brown and yellow. They seemed to go together, except that Brown looked porky and Gail smart.

"Imamu," Gail said, apologizing for her presence there. "I kept thinking of what we talked about and how you kept calling Gleaner the executor of the estate, when he was really the trustee. I phoned to tell you. But you wouldn't listen to me. So I called Brown."

He had been angry when she called, knowing she wanted to talk about the case. He hadn't wanted to talk about the case with her.

"The difference?" Imamu asked.

"The difference is, Jones," Brown said, "as trustee, Gleaner had the right to invest the Maldoon trust, but not for himself. He's been into that money for years. The latest deal, with developers who want to take over the Maldoon estate. He's practically sold the place. And it ain't his to sell. It kept bothering me, Jones. Why wait so long to get his sick sister to make a will? Your girl here put her finger on it—bright girl. I checked it out. It's true. Sophia Maldoon couldn't abrogate old Maldoon's will.

"So outside of the emotional thing, it didn't matter to Gleaner about his sister dying. Gleaner would still have his hands in the till."

"I don't get it," Imamu said.

"What he means, Imamu," Gail said, "is that Gleaner wouldn't have wanted Margaret dead."

"That's right." Otis Brown smiled. "Margaret Maldoon had complete confidence in her uncle. She was invalid, unhappy, he was her one source of strength. Gleaner knew his sister was dying. He needed Margaret Maldoon alive."

"I seen him getting arrested," Imamu said.

"For embezzlement, Jones, embezzlement. I turned all that stuff over to the DA."

"So—what are you getting at?" Imamu didn't like the expression of Gail's bright, I-am-intelligent face, or Brown's sorry-that's-the-way-it-is thick jowls. Instinctively he didn't agree with what they were going to say. And it had nothing to do with them trying to put one over. Nevertheless he asked:

"So—who do you think . . . ?"

"Old Maldoon had two grandchildren, Imamu," Gail said. A sudden flush brought a rush of blood to Imamu's head. He stiffened. But Gail kept on. "Eloise Darcy, who else? She's the one who profits from Margaret Maldoon's death."

"You know what?" Imamu said. "Both of you are damn fools."

Imamu's head was still burning when he arrived at the estate. Their betrayal was the least of it. Gail had to keep trying to prove he was no big-time detective. Her one-track mind led to one place: Education was the one thing that paid off. But Brown! That thug! That thickheaded-pea-brain-two-faced thug. How had she roped him in? How had he let her? Did Otis Brown ever solve a case when he, Imamu Jones, wasn't around to help him?

Eloise Darcy. Accusing Eloise Darcy! What did they know? About people? About anything? Gail knew her books and Brown thought he knew about power over people—the wrong people.

Imamu had expected to see Giuseppe working in the gardens, with Chips alongside. Neither were around. Dismounting at the back door, he rang the bell. When no one answered, he pushed it open and went into the kitchen. It was empty. He went back into the corridor to knock at Amanda's door.

"Come in," a small voice called out. Imamu opened the door and went in to find Amanda lying in bed, an ice bag on her head. "Oh, is you, Imamu? Oh, God, but I glad to see you, yes. I sick, sick, sick. They come and pick poor Chips up and take him away."

"Chips?" Imamu stood beside the bed looking down at her. Even in misery Amanda was handsome. Her long nose, high cheekbones, the way her hair hung around her shoulders made her look the fallen Indian chief.

"Why Chips?" Imamu asked.

"Gleaner," Amanda said. "The police arrest him and it's he accuse the boy. He say he chase Chips away from Margaret that day. He even relate to them about Chips liking to peep.

"It's because they catch him good thiefing," Amanda said. "Can you imagine, the executor of the estate and thiefing all the time—but I told you."

"Trustee," Imamu corrected her.

"Executor, trustee, all the same thing. He a thief. He get in trouble and trying to bring everybody down with him. He say Chips is dangerous."

"Did the police say what Chips's motive is?"

"Ain't it rape they want to say? They say Margaret wouldn't let him—so he throw her in the pool."

"Chair and all?" Imamu asked, thinking of Chips's strength. But if Chips wanted to rape poor, weak Margaret there would be no contest.

"It look bad, Imamu," Amanda cried. "Brown now saying that Giuseppe and me hide Chips to obstruct justice. But Chips got his own place he does go. He can hide us. We can't hide him." Tears rolled down the sides of her face into the pillow.

Seeing strong Amanda cry made Imamu helpless. "Brown's a fool," he said. "When did they take him?"

"Yesterday. Poor Giuseppe. He in town to be near the boy. Chips ain't never been so far away from here. What to do, Imamu? Poor Margaret—gone. Sophia—gone. Miss Norris—gone. Now Chips and Giuseppe. Did you ever see a place change so?"

How to comfort her? Remind her that Charlotte Darcy was still there? That she was still here? What good would that do? She loved Chips. She had raised him. Giuseppe had been her friend for forty years. What could he offer to compare?

"Isn't there something you want me to help you with, Amanda?"

"Where to start with so much to do?"

"I can open up the windows—take out the garbage."

"Oh, Imamu, but you're a good boy, yes. A sweetheart," Amanda said, and smiled again.

Imamu went into the parlor, opened the blinds, and stood looking out at the table beneath the great elm, and over the spreading lawn. The place had the feel of being deserted—a ghost city where all occupants had died. He thought of Eloise, her open face, her intelligent eyes. Was no one sacred in this case? Did they all have to suffer Brown—the fool, fool, fool?

Imamu imagined the house abandoned. He imagined he heard, from the second floor, window slats banging in the wind. A haunted house. It would be, for him.

Yet Charlotte Darcy was still there. Upstairs, in her blue room, searching through her blue wardrobe for the suitable clothes with which to wander through the almost empty house.

Leaving the window, Imamu walked from the living room across the hall to the stairs. He started to walk up, but changing his mind, went out of the front door, across the lawn, across the concrete path, and into Giuseppe's garden.

Most of the tulips, full-grown, had lost their petals. Choosing the best among those remaining, he made a small bouquet and retraced his steps to the house.

In the hall he stood remembering eyes that bored holes in his back. He waited, wanting the ghosts once again to surround him, to haunt him, to remember him. But only the ghosts of the recent dead flittered around searching, demanding their places in that gallery.

Where were the portraits of Margaret? Where was the likeness of Sophia Maldoon? Were there no places for them? Were they to drift forever up and down the stairs, through the empty rooms, around the table in the lawn, down to the pool, never finding their niches among the Maldoons?

Imamu walked up the stairs, his heart almost suffocating him. It beat hard in his chest, then leaped to beat in his throat. He went directly to her room, clutching the bouquet to his bosom, little-boy fashion. She would be surprised. Yet she must have been expecting him—at some time—after all her encouragement.

She had to know that he kept his promise—the promise in his eyes. Through all his fears, his nightmares, he had this one constant thought. And now he had come, finally, to bring her her flowers.

He knocked lightly, and the door opened to the

pressure of his hand. Careless. Disappointed, for he had thought to tap lightly, listen to her call, then enter surprising her. Now he entered, closed the door behind him, and instantly felt uneasy. He had no right to close her open door—unless she invited him to.

But the house was empty, except for Amanda, sick in her room below. He left the door closed—a precaution against Amanda's sudden return to good health.

He looked around at the disorder of the room—clothes scattered about, her bed unmade. The unmade bed gave Imamu a start, a burning face, a sudden closeness to Charlotte Darcy that he wasn't prepared for.

Going to the dresser, he examined the photograph, with its arrangement of now wilted flowers. Her husband, this tall, slim, handsome man, with almost white hair. *Dapper, carefree, fun-loving, aristocratic, but poor,* Amanda had said.

Charlotte had loved him. Imamu picked up the picture, searching for resemblances, but replaced it immediately as the bathroom door opened.

A gust of humid air moistened the back of his neck, clouded the mirror where she suddenly appeared. They stared at each other through the mirror and Imamu, startled by the terror widening her eyes, turned, and took a step toward her shaking his head, he meant her no harm. Then, remembering the flowers, he held them out to her. She stared over the flowers, into his eyes. He let them drop to the floor and took a backward step, still shaking his head.

He wished her dressed. He wished her in her blue, long-sleeved dress. He wished her too thin arms, her slackened skin, covered. He wished to apologize for having dared to see her so—uncovered.

But the terror in her eyes had vanished. The crinkles at their corners recalled their smile. "A delivery boy . . ." she said, with a barely perceptible shake of her head.

A sudden heat, starting at his feet, rushed through Imamu. It stretched him tall, expanded his chest, threatened the barrier of his shirt, thickened the muscles in his arms. "A black delivery boy . . ." Charlotte Darcy said, and the muscles twitched over Imamu's entire body.

Vapor rising through his eyes filled the space between them. It framed her small body, underlined its helplessness, her nakedness. There she stood in the shadow of his might—a thing, a thing needing to be crushed. Sweat broke out on his head. Water gushed down the sides of his face. He backed to the door, reached for the knob.

The knob, the knob, where the hell was that damn fool doorknob! His hand touched the round coldness, fumbled. She laughed. He wrenched the door open, ran from the room, and kept on running.

20

On the stairs to his apartment, he heard the phone ringing. He opened the door, and hot, sweaty, agitated, he dashed past it to his room. But seeing his mother approaching to answer, he snatched the phone from its cradle and shouted: "Yeah?"

"Well, laddie," a voice boomed. "What's happening with you? I've been expecting you."

The voice, from another time, another place, another world, added to his agitation. Imamu knew he should connect the voice to a body, but his agitation didn't allow it. "Who? Me? Why me?"

"Sure. Laddie, you know you're the best boy I ever had. Now that the police say that you're cleared . . ."

"Cleared?" Then he knew it was McDermott. Had he really been cleared? Who had they nailed in his stead? Chips? Eloise?

"Yes, lad, you're cleared. When will you be coming in?"

"I'll be in, Mr. McDermott," Imamu said. But did he really want to? "Soon."

"Tomorrow?" McDermott asked.

"Tomorrow?" Imamu repeated. Then he thought of the days he had gone from the house to walk, restless, around the streets, the park, waiting for this call. "Not tomorrow."

"But when, laddie? I'm needing you."

"I'll call you—let you know. . . ." He hung up.

Soon? How soon was soon? He had loved the big guy. Seeing him bow to James Gleaner had killed that love. The thrill of working for McDermott the man, McDermott's the big gourmet shop, was gone.

Imamu turned and collided with his mother in the doorway. He ducked around her and went into his room. She wanted to talk. Her face quivered with her need to talk. What to say to this woman whose life touched him, was woven so tightly through his, yet was far removed from his smallest dreams? And what were those dreams that could include her? He no longer had any dreams—and he was so young.

Indeed, Imamu felt himself being pulled in too many ways. Pulled into manhood, while still needing the protection that childhood offered. He needed to be the small boy again—tiny, dependent, the child his father had left behind, clinging to somebody. Her? She had so long ceased being the mother.

She stood in the doorway, still wanting to talk. "That was your boss?" she asked.

Imamu nodded yes. He didn't want to talk. He didn't want to understand all things, this day. He needed more than anything to be understood.

"You ain't been working, Son?" she asked.

Imamu sat at the edge of the bed, staring at the floor from between his knees. "Something done happen?" He kept staring at the floor. "What's troubling you, Son? Gail?"

Imamu shook his head, not Gail.

"No, not Gail," she said, agreeing.

Why did she bother? Why didn't she just leave and go on into her room, this wino woman whom he had cared for, still cared for, was destined to care for —forever.

Guilt, because he felt burdened by her. He looked up to apologize and saw—with a shock—her eyes looking back into his! He saw, too, that her face had lost its twitch! "Can we talk about it, Son?" she said.

They had talked about so little in their lives. They seemed never to have had the ability to communicate. "I don't want to talk to nobody, Moma," Imamu said.

"You going through some mighty troublesome times, Son. It's tearing you to pieces—inside. Try me. I've gone through some changes too."

The steadiness in her faded eyes held.

"Lots have happened, Moma," he said. He lay

back across the bed, hands beneath his head, and stared up at the ceiling.

"Must have," she agreed.

"This guy I work for—let me down." Tears thickened his throat. He tried to swallow them before they reached his eyes.

"More'n I let you down?"

"I had faith in him."

"More'n you had in me?"

Imamu held silent. To deny it would put a question mark around why they were in this house, in Brooklyn, instead of their broken-down Harlem flat. To agree would be to lie. "Different, Moma," he said. "Different.

"There was this girl. She needed me. I had made her a sort of promise . . ."

"And?" She kept probing, kept pushing him, relentlessly. She needed to understand.

"She needed me, Moma. And I didn't keep my promise to her."

"Because you had to be here—with me?"

"Guess so."

"But that was important, too, Son. Couldn't be but in one place at a time, now—could you?"

She was trying. God knows she was trying. She had been his worry, his reason for all things so long. His mother. And if he wanted, he could make her the perfect excuse—for anything.

"I could have made arrangements, Moma. But there was this man. A prejudice son of a bitch."

Imamu's voice grew hoarse in his hatred. "He was mad that I was even around. . . ."

"Talking about that Maldoon affair, ain't you, Son?"

Imamu nodded, confused, angry. He knew he had brought back that pound of butter as an act of defiance. "He's evil, Moma," Imamu said, still defiant. "Evil enough to kill. . . ."

"Because he was prejudice?"

Imamu jerked his head up to stare at his mother. He shook his head no. And after a few more seconds had ticked by, he was able to answer: "No."

"Talking about that poor girl what been drowned?" Mrs. Jones asked.

"Yes," Imamu cried, still wanting to hold on to his crumbling theories. "He wanted to blame me. Said I raped her. He wanted me dead, Moma. I never done him nothing, yet he wanted me dead. He cost me my job, Moma. He caused McDermott to lay me off."

"That where you been going, mornings when you leave outa here? To try to get even?"

"No! To find out the truth," Imamu cried. "I wanted him—"

He almost said dead. But had that really to do with his thinking? "I wanted the truth," he repeated. But his mother had understood.

"Don't work that way, Son," she said. She sat down beside him. "Remember how when the law got to be putting you away for stealing, how mad I'd be

—at you? Even when they accused you of things—
like the disappearance of the little Aimsley gal. I
swore out you did it.

"Anyway, if even you hadn't done the things they
said, I thought you'd be better off in jail, than on the
streets and end up killing, or getting killed.

"Lord, John, that's a mighty heavy weight for a
son to carry. The world against him and his mother
too. . . .

"Ain't making no excuse. It done happened. Your
daddy gone, me not able to stop him going. Having
to care for you and knowing nothing I wanted for
you, I could make happen. No money, no education.
Just a black woman out there whose man done been
took away—and weak. . . .

"John, it's the wicked what rules the world. They
seems to have you when you trying to move ahead,
or when you standing still. They don't have to do
one thing but hate. But it's when they got you hating
like them that they knows they gotcha . . ."

Imamu heard her moving around in the kitchen.
He heard her words. Her words forced him up from
the bed. Going to the closet, he searched through
clothes that he had let fall carelessly to the floor. At
the bottom of the heap he found the jeans he had
been searching for. They were bunched up into a
hardened ball from being tossed there wet.

Pressing the pants out on the bed, Imamu went
through the stiffened pockets. He found it. The

handkerchief—her handkerchief. Taking it, he put it to his nose and inhaled, pulling her familiar lavender scent through him. Putting it into his pocket, he went to the kitchen for his bicycle.

"John." His mother stopped him at the door. She had been looking into her green window box. "I know you could have had a good life with the Aimsleys," she said. "If you hadn't looked back for me . . . If you hadn't, I'd have been long dead and you free. . . ."

So she did understand his resentment, his guilt. "Instead, you picked up this poor old lady from off the streets, poured your strength into her talking about being perfect . . . About me growing the perfect flower. Hee-hee." She laughed at the joke of it. Then she beckoned him. "Come here, John Jones, and see."

Imamu walked over to her. "You been so tied up inside yourself here lately, you ain't even stopped to see how I been doing. But look . . ."

Imamu looked into the box. A little red flower had pushed up through the green shoots that a few days before, Gail had mistaken for weeds. "Now, if this ain't the most perfect flower in the world . . . God sure don't know what perfect means. . . ."

21

For the first time since he had been coming to the estate, Imamu found no sunshine at the other end of the tunnel. Clouds had gathered to shade the light of the sun. The hill did not glow golden; rather, the somber landscape seemed—as it must have been once—an extension of the woods. Imamu rode through the gate, a chill descending over him.

Had it been only hours since he had come to find Amanda, in her room sick? Had it been only hours since he stood in the upstairs bedroom looking at— or trying not to—the naked Charlotte Darcy and had reacted to the expression on her face, even more than to her nakedness?

April rains would fall on the Maldoon estate after all—rains never needed where birds twittered and pecked in the gold of the sun, and where perfect flowers bloomed anyway—unnatural.

It had seemed so. It was as unnatural as the horrors he had lived through: as eerie as fishing a body out of the pool—a cold, hard, dead-as-a-rat body. As nightmarish as being attacked by the wild, unfriendly woods, only to discover the woods more real and that he was the one hallucinating. Certainly as unnatural as being strangled, staring into the eyes of a woman—as she died.

Imamu intended to go right to the front door. Habit forced him to the back. Habit and perhaps a reluctance to let go—to end the dream.

"Oh-ho," Amanda greeted him. "But where you went to this morning? I look for you everywhere. How you go off so and don't tell me?"

"Had to," Imamu said. "Feeling better now?"

"Oh, yes, man. God, you ain't know how much."

The sparkle had come back to her eyes and with it the house had sprung to life. "Imamu, things start to happen. A new maid come today. I wanted for you to meet her, but you had gone. Soon we'll be getting a new cook. I'll be housekeeper."

Imamu looked around the spotless kitchen. Its cleanliness, its untouched-by-tragedy look, solidified the chill through him.

"What about Chips?" he asked.

"Chips coming home. Giuseppe just call. But how they can hold him? He ain't do nothing. Is that Gleaner . . ."

"Where's Mrs. Darcy?" Imamu asked.

"In the living room—with Eloise," Amanda said.

So they hadn't picked her up—yet. Thank God. He headed for the door. "What?" Amanda protested. "You ain't want to hear the rest? Come nuh, sweetheart. Help me peel potatoes."

Imamu kept on going. He no longer wanted to hear. Perhaps it was because of the spotless kitchen, but the dream—the Maldoon fable—had ended.

He left by the back door and going around to the front, pushed the door open. Almost immediately a young woman approached. She wore a maid's uniform—frilled white cap, a white apron over a black dress.

"I came to see Mrs. Darcy," Imamu said.

"Whom shall I say is calling?"

Imamu pushed past her. He hadn't come to play games.

Walking toward the living room, he heard Eloise Darcy say: "Mother, it's obscene the way you're rushing things."

"My God, Eloise," Charlotte Darcy answered. "Hasn't this house been in mourning long enough? Haven't we all suffered?"

"Mother, it's impossible to maintain this oversize house. When his case is heard, I'm sure Uncle James will sell."

"Your uncle James Gleaner is no longer in the position to do anything about this house—or this property," Charlotte Darcy said, laughing.

"He's to be acquitted," Eloise said. "What has he

done, except in Aunt Sophia and Margaret's interest."

"Eloise, you don't understand. James is a criminal. He has fraudulently abused the Maldoon—your —trust for his benefit. He's going to jail and there's nothing he, or you, or anyone can do to stop it."

"Then I'll sell," Eloise said.

"My, you certainly did inherit your father's utter lack of responsibility. Have you thought about me? Or do you care what happens to me?"

"Mother, you'll always be cared for."

"In our house, Eloise. Our home." She looked past Eloise and saw Imamu standing in the doorway.

Her anger, her hostility, was easily camouflaged by the crinkles that held her smile firmly in the corners of her eyes. Sitting in the wing chair, she appeared calm, regal in her long-sleeved blue dress, her hair twisted in its bun.

This is the way she should look, always, Imamu thought. This is the way I wish I could remember her. Charlotte Darcy waited for him to speak. But when Eloise saw him, she got up and came to the door, holding out her hand.

"Imamu Jones." Her face was red from the angry exchange with her mother. "How good of you to come. I had hoped to see you at the funeral. When I didn't, I supposed we wouldn't meet again."

Imamu held on to her hand. He was glad she was here. Glad, too, he had come before Brown had had a chance to get to her.

"Most likely we won't meet—after today," he said.

Regret sounded in his voice, reflected in his eyes. Eloise reached for her bag on the coffee table. Taking out a card, she handed it to Imamu. "Not unless we want to," she said. "I do. Call me—whenever you like. Whenever you feel like talking."

"Touching," Charlotte Darcy said. "I take it, then, it's my daughter you came to renew your acquaintance with, Imamu Jones."

"No," Imamu answered, putting the card in his pocket. "I came to talk to you."

"What about?"

"Alone," he said.

"What can you possibly have to say to me that can't be said in the presence of my daughter?" Relieved that she had rejected the chance he had given her from courtesy, Imamu took the handkerchief from his pocket and laid it on the coffee table in front of her. "Your handkerchief, Mrs. Darcy," he said.

"My—handkerchief . . . ?" She looked down at the wrinkled square, blue-embroidered cloth. Hers and hers alone. But she didn't move to pick it up. "Mine?"

"Yes, Mrs. Darcy—yours."

Reluctantly she reached for it, put it in her lap, and pressed out the wrinkles. "Where did you—find it—up in my room, no doubt?"

Well done. With nerve. With finesse—all meant to

point up to Eloise his indiscretion. "No, Mrs. Darcy," Imamu said flatly. "I found that handkerchief on the slope leading down to the pool—that Friday morning. The morning I found Margaret. You dropped it—when you pushed the wheelchair down the hill."

"That's not true," Charlotte Darcy said. "You stole it—from my room." But the handkerchief on her lap wrinkled up, making ugly faces.

"When?" Imamu asked. "You mean when I went up to your room to rape you?"

Saying it out gave the lie to it, made it sound implausible. There were no secrets—there never had been. "Why should I want to rape you? If I had asked, you'd have given willingly—wouldn't you?"

Silence fell over the room. A long silence so profound, it threatened their eardrums. Charlotte Darcy's eyes grew a deeper—almost dark—blue. Still the crinkles at their corners held their smile. She pushed herself deeper into the contours of the chair. Imamu looked into her mind. She had a choice: accuse him of rape and so strengthen Gleaner's accusations. But did that prove murder?

Imamu let the silence go on. He had already let it go on too long. To protect her? To get James Gleaner? Or had he been willfully blind—to what now was so obvious, what had been obvious from the first—anxious to tie this street cat to the big dream, her big dream?

As though she, too, was listening to his thoughts,

Charlotte Darcy laughed. "You delivery boys do take yourselves seriously. James had the right approach. Keep them in their place."

Imamu's ears burned. He waited, but there was no repetition of the deadly anger that had forced him to run from her earlier.

"Then Mrs. Darcy, you'd never have had me to use," Imamu said.

It had come through clear to him as she stood before him naked, confused: *a delivery boy . . . a black delivery boy . . .*

How does it happen that I, elegant, charming— lady of the manor, blond queen in everyone's fairy tale, I whom servants are supposed to bow to, give their lives for willingly—have in my bedroom a delivery boy? And he can rape me at will!

She looked at Imamu now, not understanding how a black delivery boy could undo plans so long in the preparations. Plans made long before he had arrived on the scene. Plans made even before the weatherman had decreed it be a hotter than usual April.

Imamu remembered the flowers. The pound of butter. Butter *she* had to have. The butter Amanda had demanded he bring back. He was to have brought it back that evening. But it hadn't worked. James Gleaner, McDermott, had blown it.

When it turned out that he knew Detective Otis Brown: "Aren't you clever"; "James is so violent. James chased Chips . . ." Leading. Leading. But he had wanted to be led! He had offered himself. She had seduced him. But he had wanted to be seduced! *A . . . a delivery boy . . .* It could have been *any delivery boy!*

"What do you intend to do about it, Imamu Jones? Report back to your Detective Brown? Or are you going to bring me in?"

"I ain't the law, Mrs. Darcy," Imamu said. "The reason I'm here today is because my old lady reminded me that I'm different. I'm about caring. It's about murder and you got to pay."

"How amusing," Charlotte Darcy said. "Now you're the judge."

"No ma'am. Just a delivery boy," Imamu said.

"Just a delivery boy," Charlotte Darcy mimicked. She picked up the handkerchief. "Who couldn't forget this delivery?"

"No ma'am, I can't," Imamu said.

"Mother, do you know what you're saying!" Eloise cried.

"Yes, Eloise, I know exactly what I'm saying! I'm asking Imamu Jones to withhold evidence."

"I can't believe this," Eloise said. "How dare you!"

"Eloise, this all started long before you were born. It's between James Gleaner and me. . . .

"James Gleaner, bringing his sister into *my* house. James Gleaner turning *my* father against me—against your father, Eloise.

"Before he came, my father had never been able to

hold anything against me. He loved me. I worshiped him. He didn't like your father but in time I could have made him.

"Scheming James Gleaner. Your grandfather was so anxious to spite me for marrying your father. That gave James his big chance. How easy to tie weak Daniel to sweet-sickly Sophia—with pity. So he brought her around and—*voilà*. Father admired strength. He respected James—admired his rags-to-riches drive. When Sophia and Dan got married, James, the trusted lawyer, became son, executor of his will, the trustee of the estate.

"James Gleaner's ambitions fulfilled!

"Long before your uncle died, Eloise, James was manipulating the trust. He invested heavily. After the accident, he didn't even have to give an accounting. Sophia trusted and worshiped him, and Margaret—what could she do?

"I don't know how much he invested, or how much he lost. But he did lose. Then came this chance—a multimillion-dollar chance. Turn the Maldoon estate into a condominium, with its malls —a city within a city, really—and become the untouchably rich lawyer. Gambling with your future. Did he think I'd sit back and allow that?

"Did James Gleaner think we Maldoons maintained our standards through the years by letting trash like him scheme and outwit us? They're a different breed, Eloise."

"Mother," Eloise said, not understanding what her mother was saying. "Margaret was your niece."

"Sophia was dying—ever since she came to this house, really." Charlotte Darcy, too, seemed insensible to all but her own inner thoughts. "She had the stroke, still she kept hanging on.

"But even if Sophia died there was always Margaret. He was her uncle James, always in charge, always keeping the house going. Eloise, can you imagine, that passive creature mistress of the Maldoon estate? They both had to die!"

"Mother, you're mad," Eloise cried.

"Margaret helped. Her fear of Chips. I suspect she was pretending to get attention. She always wanted attention. What she succeeded in doing was getting James to bar Chips, the one who might have protected her, from the grounds.

"Thursday, I saw Chips going down to clean the pool. I told James. He did what I expected. He chased Chips away, then went looking for Giuseppe —the ritual . . .

"I went downstairs, picked up the bust of my father . . ." She laughed. "Justice—and poetry, and all of that . . . I went outside and struck Margaret on her head."

"No, no," Eloise cried.

"She never saw me, Eloise. I struck her unconscious—she never regained consciousness.

"I pushed the wheelchair down the hill into the water. Then I went up to Sophia. 'Sophia,' I said. 'I know you've been waiting for a long time for this. Margaret's dead. She just killed herself.'

"Sophia was so weak from her last stroke, how could she stand up . . . ?"

"You killed them both!" Eloise said, her body shaking.

"But she kept hanging on. And almost upset my plans.

"James was desperate after Margaret died. He knew he had me—had us—to deal with. Only Sophia's signature, taking full responsibility for his crime, might have saved him. A criminal. That's what he is. What he's always been.

"And Sophia would have signed. She knew—I had told her—Margaret was dead. With the last breath of her body she had to try to save her brother.

"But by a miracle, Imamu happened to be in the house, at that moment.

"They deserved to die, Eloise," Charlotte Darcy said. "We Maldoons have never been known to flinch from protecting what's ours."

"Mother, Margaret was a Maldoon too," Eloise said.

"Nonsense, Eloise, Margaret was Sophia's daughter—James Gleaner's niece. You're the true Maldoon. The estate now is yours."

"No, Mother, I'm a Darcy. This house had always been inhospitable to the Darcys. I hate it. I want to see it destroyed."

"You are mad," Charlotte Darcy said.

"No, Mother, I am not mad. . . ."

Imamu left them then. He stopped in the hall and looked around at the busts, the portraits—the ghosts of times past. Then he went to the kitchen to use the phone to call Detective Otis Brown.

22

He'd never be back. Never see the mansion or its grounds, which for a short time had seemed the doorway to dreams he had been willing to spend his energies—meaning his life—to gain. Now the clouds hung low, shutting off the sky. The lawn appeared dull, brown, burned by the intense rays of sun.

Imamu looked over at the lawn sloping steeply down to the dell—the pool. He imagined a hand—weak, crippled, rising out of the void, its finger pointing, accusing him. . . .

But how could he have helped her? She whose death had been set up so long before she was born? So long before he—black boy, with a simple grin, blinded by the gold of the sun—had raced his bicycle into her life.

The delivery boy, the delivery boy out of the

streets, with the word *perfection* so new to his mind
—it might have been stuck there with spit and chewing gum—feeding her promises he had no power to
keep.

She had felt danger. She had been in danger. Danger lurked all around her—from eyes peering down,
keeping her forever in sight, forever victim. Tears
blinded Imamu. He raced through the gates and
down the stretch of forested road. Now his bike
didn't go fast enough. He had to get somewhere, talk
to somebody.

He rode to the gourmet shop. But when he looked
into the window and saw McDermott's big red head
bent over the counter, he sped on. Moma? She had
been great that morning. He headed home. Again
his bicycle sped on. He found himself stopping in
front of the Aimsleys' brownstone.

Peter Aimsley was home. His car, parked at the
curb. Yet, when Gail let him in and Imamu saw his
foster father sitting in his chair, in front of the television set, in the living room, he flew into a silent rage.

He wanted to talk—but to Gail. He needed the
entire house to talk to her, to argue with her, to tell
her she was wrong, wrong, and in some perverse
way tease her, chase her, shout at her. And he
wanted to hear her big-talking, superior know-it-all
answers. He wanted to laugh with her. But more, he
wanted to cry.

Imamu put a toothpick in his mouth. He sat next
to Gail on the couch, brooding. Worse, the smell of

chicken frying came up from the kitchen. Soon Mrs. Aimsley would be calling them down for dinner. Imamu wanted to shout, scream, throw himself at the television and kick it. He bit hard on the toothpick.

Of course, he wouldn't. No more than he would cry. Tears choked him. Tears came up to his eyes. He blinked them down. He wasn't that kind of dude. Restless, impatient, he jumped to his feet, walked over to look at his painting on the wall. Staring into the roaring surf, Imamu imagined he heard the pain of the painter crying out. He saw among the little matchstick figures, the finger, once again, pointing at him, accusing him.

Imamu swallowed, trying to push the lump back from his throat. He took a toothpick from his mouth, looked around for an ashtray, and when he didn't see one, crumpled the toothpick in his fist and headed for the door.

"Hey, you just got here," Gail said. She jumped up, ran after him, and grabbed his arm before he reached the front door. "You can't come in and walk out without saying anything."

"Why?" he asked, being unreasonable and knowing it. "Because this ain't my house?"

"We didn't do it," Gail said, getting angry. "Whatever was done to you isn't our fault."

"What kind of talk is that?" Peter Aimsley said from his seat in front of the television set. "You come in here with a chip on your behind? Well, I'm the one to knock it off." He spoke half jokingly but dead serious. "Come on back in here, boy, and sit down. If something's wrong, if we did something to upset you, just say it."

Imamu walked back to stand in the doorway, looking down at Peter Aimsley. He looked comfortable, in his chair, his slippered feet on a hassock, his fingers joined over his lean, hard stomach.

"Why do you do it, Mr. Aimsley?" Imamu asked.

"Do what, man?"

"Work like hell?"

Peter Aimsley's head snapped up. He lowered it to stare at the television. " 'Cause I like to," he said.

That gave Imamu a start. He had expected the man to make excuses: because of his family; his daughter had to be put through school; the house needed this, it needed that. Imamu realized suddenly that he had never heard his foster father complain about work.

"You mean you like that hard work? You like coming home with your hands so dirty they can't ever become clean?" Imamu waited, expecting Peter Aimsley to stand up, square off, ready to give him a knocking around. He expected to be asked to leave.

Peter Aimsley looked down at his hands—back and front. He seemed surprised to find the line of darkness beneath his nails. He rubbed his fingernails against his pant leg, then looked at them again. "Yeah, that's right," he said. "Man's got to do something to take up time while he's around. Me, I like being around—working.

"I takes my li'l trips to the islands, once in a while. But I ain't too much into swimming. I like winter. Don't ski. Too old to try. But work . . ." He nodded. "I know how to work. I do good work and don't get tired. I'd die if I retired—so . . .

"Ann's grown. Got more education than me. She can look out for herself. If push comes to shove, her daughter there"—he indicated Gail with his chin— "can go out and hustle. She's old enough, and more, her head's on straighter than mine ever was. I can sell my business tomorrow and get more than enough to last me till I die. And if I die, Ann and Gail can sell—and they got my insurance too. So I got to like it, or I wouldn't be doing it—right?

"Yep," Peter Aimsley said. "I loves getting up mornings, loves seeing the seasons change. Loves to see that birds got nothing on me when I hear them chirping early in the morning—because I'm awake too. I like the feeling of that hunk of metal jumping to life, under the pressure of my big toe. Makes me feel mighty powerful—important. I can't change the world, but when I makes that sucker roar, I got the feeling I can."

Imamu took another toothpick and put it into his mouth. He stared down at Peter Aimsley. He liked his answer. The answer had nothing to do with Mrs. Aimsley or Gail—only with Peter Aimsley. And that's what it was all about. Moma had heard a bird singing—and it had nothing to do with that perfect flower.

"Okay," Imamu said, nodding. "Okay." He walked to the door.

"Hold it, boy," Peter Aimsley shouted. "You come right back here and tell me what the hell's eating you." And because his foster father had raised his voice, had ordered him, Imamu walked back— the little lost boy.

"I don't know," he said.

"Well, it's something," Peter Aimsley said. "Talk about it—try."

"I—I . . ." The tears, so near the surface, brimmed over. They ran down his cheeks. Imamu tried to wipe them. Couldn't. He covered his face with his hands and let them flow. Sobs punished his throat. Yes. He wanted to talk. Oh, God, how he needed to tell somebody.

He wanted to talk about Margaret Maldoon. He wasn't to blame for her death. He had broken his promise—but she had been doomed to die. He wanted to discuss finding her—her hard, cold body, the hands. But her hands had been helpless even before she had died. She had begged: *Come back, come back. . . .* But it hadn't been his fault.

He wanted to talk about power. Real power. He had known real power. He had felt it in Charlotte Darcy's room. He had been so powerful, he could have made her his victim. But if he had crushed her, wouldn't he be victim too?

"I got a good mind," he shouted in his own defense. "A real good mind. I know it! I can tell what folks is thinking almost before they think it.

"I *let* myself be used," he cried. "I wanted folks to see me, to look at me for what I am. But nobody sees me. I'm nothing.

"Here I am eighteen years old and my life's finished. I don't have nothing. Know why? Because my life was done before I was born. I was born in the wrong place—from wrong folks." Imamu broke off, sobbing.

"What's the matter, Imamu?" Gail came to him and put her arm around his back to support him. She was crying, and that made his tears flow even faster.

"But you know what?" he heard himself shouting. "Moma heard a bird sing . . ." So she was well again, could go for herself again, and he was out there by himself again. "Moma heard a bird sing," he repeated, trying to laugh.

"Because of you," Gail said. Imamu shook his head and Gail insisted. "Yes, Imamu, because you're the perfect son. I love you, Imamu Jones—so please, please stop. . . ."

Her tears wet his neck. And that's what he had wanted. Her. He needed her. He wanted her to cry with him—for him. She was his. His only friend. He wanted to lean against her small, shapely, strong frame. She was his bigmouthed Gail.

Peter Aimsley remained silent. Why? Why did his

foster father let him cry, looking on as though he and Gail were a pair of clowns escaped from a soap opera? "Look," Imamu said, "I got to go now."

But Peter Aimsley's heavy hand had replaced Gail's across his back. "Boy, something's bothering you. You're not going back in the streets in that state. You come here to talk. And you the only one been talking. . . .

"Yeah, you got a good mind. A damn good mind. At least as good as those around this house. I know Gail gives you hell about this and that, and Ann's always saying this and that. But that don't mean they got anything on us when it come to thinking.

"I agree with you, son," Peter Aimsley said. "It's time to start thinking about how you gonna develop your future and what you gonna do with that good mind.

"What better time to start? Your mother's coming on fine. You done what you set out to do. That ain't no little thing, boy. So now go for yourself."

"How do I start? Where do I go? I'm eighteen— almost nineteen—and don't have no education."

"But as you say—you got a good mind," Peter Aimsley reminded Imamu. "Don't forget that. Never forget that. At your age—at any age. Once you got that together, it's time to start."

"With what? What do I use for money? I'm just a delivery boy."

"Ain't nothing wrong with that—unless you don't like delivering. But what's wrong with auto repairs, except that it's bound to get your hands—damn dirty." He smiled to take guilt away from Imamu. "I got a place for a boy who don't mind getting his hands dirty. Part time. I don't mind paying you wages and paying for your schooling too."

"You? Pay for me? Why?"

"Because you're my son."

Imamu took in a quick breath. He heard that. He heard it deep inside. The barrier between his foster father and himself had kept them from ever really talking. But now he heard him. "Let's put it this way, Imamu. If you had stayed on here like a son, instead of running off to take care of your mother, like a man, it would have cost me a hell of a lot more just to feed you—the way you eat. So, the way I see it, I'm getting off damn cheap."

Imamu wanted to protest, to say no like a man ought to. Why should this man, a stranger who had been pulled into his life by his wife and daughter, want to help him? "Anyway," Peter Aimsley went on, "what kind of man you think me? Educating my girl and letting my boy drop by the wayside? Ain't that reverse discrimination, Gail?"

"Sounds like it to me, Daddy," Gail agreed.

"He mean it?" Imamu whispered to Gail.

"Imamu, your father never says anything he doesn't mean," Gail answered.

"But why now?" he asked. "Why not before?"

"You're ready now," Peter Aimsley said. "Nothing worse than shoving something down a feller's throat that he ain't ready to digest. Don't matter if it's for his good, he'd end up spitting it back up."

Imamu wiped his face and nose on his sleeve. "Gotta go now," he said. "Gotta tell Moma. Tell Mrs. Aimsley that I'll—that we'll be back for some of that good fried chicken."

Gail, her arm around Imamu, walked with him out to the stoop. "Everything will be just fine, Imamu. I know it will."

"But Gail, if I go to school, that'll mean I won't be able to get a real apartment until—until—"

"Why don't you aim for twenty-one, Imamu," she said.

"Okay, Sis, I hear you." Imamu hugged Gail to him. But when he ran down the steps, mounted his bike, and started off, the strange feeling at the pit of his stomach had nothing to do with her being his sister.

"That's the way I see it, Brown." Imamu looked across the desk at Brown. "Charlotte Darcy was so eaten up with hate and jealousy that Sophia Maldoon had to pay, the moment that she moved into that house, and into old Maldoon's affection. And she did."

"Charlotte Darcy has to pay too," Brown said. "Her daughter thinks that she's mad—and she may be. But the judge will have to decide that."

"If she isn't mad now, by the time Eloise goes

through with selling the house, she will be," Imamu said.

"I keep wondering," Gail said. "If any of this would have happened if Margaret hadn't made her father take her to Italy. It was the accident that killed him and crippled her that made all of this possible, isn't it?"

"Fate plays some weird games," Imamu said, thinking back to all the things that had happened since he, poor innocent, had stumbled in so near the end of the heavy drama. "Margaret being spoiled played a great part in her own death. Yet I believe the only way either Sophia, or Margaret, could have escaped certain death was to have moved away from that house.

"Neither could. They all were tied up to that house—Charlotte, Sophia, Margaret—even the cook, Amanda." And he understood. Hadn't he been captured—captivated by its mystery, its luxury, its history?

"Ought to turn you in all the same, Jones," Brown said. "Suppressing evidence. What's the big idea of turning that handkerchief over to Mrs. Darcy instead of to me?"

"Brown, if I had handed you that li'l piece of square cloth, what would you have done with it?" Imamu asked. He looked at Gail, then beyond her.

That had been his greatest guilt. . . . He had known. Somewhere deep in the middle of him, since he had found that square piece of cloth, he had known—and had refused to admit it even to himself.

"But Imamu did pull things together, Detective Brown," Gail said sweetly. "He even got a witness to the confession."

"What witness?"

"Her daughter," Imamu said, wondering if he'd ever see Eloise Darcy again. What if he called her? Would she say yes to lunch? to a talk? After he had accused her mother?

"She's been cooperating. That's because she's sure Charlotte Darcy will be found insane. You know one thing, Jones? I sure hate that it ain't the Gleaner guy. I'd love to see him put away for good."

"But he didn't do it, Brown," Imamu said. "He'll do his time for grand larceny. But he oughtn't to be serving time for something he didn't do."

"That coming from you?" Brown said. "I thought you wanted that dude under the jail."

"He will be," Imamu said, shrugging. "But I don't want to see him in for murder. I've changed."

"Youngblood, that's all I been hearing from you— change, change, change. What's that all about?"

"That's about life, Brown. Life," Imamu said. "Keeps on changing. I'm even going back to school."

"No jive," Brown said. "Your girl talk you into it?"

"Decided to be a detective," Imamu said.

"Then you ought to have your head examined," Brown said.

"Oh, not your kind of detective." Imamu dismissed that thought with a wave of his hand. ". . . With my intelligence? I'm going to study psychology and law, and . . ."

"Intelligence!" Brown barked. And Gail smiled. "What you gonna do with this turkey?" he asked her.

"Bandage up his head—tight," Gail said. "That ought to stop the swelling—and keep him out of trouble. Know what I mean?"